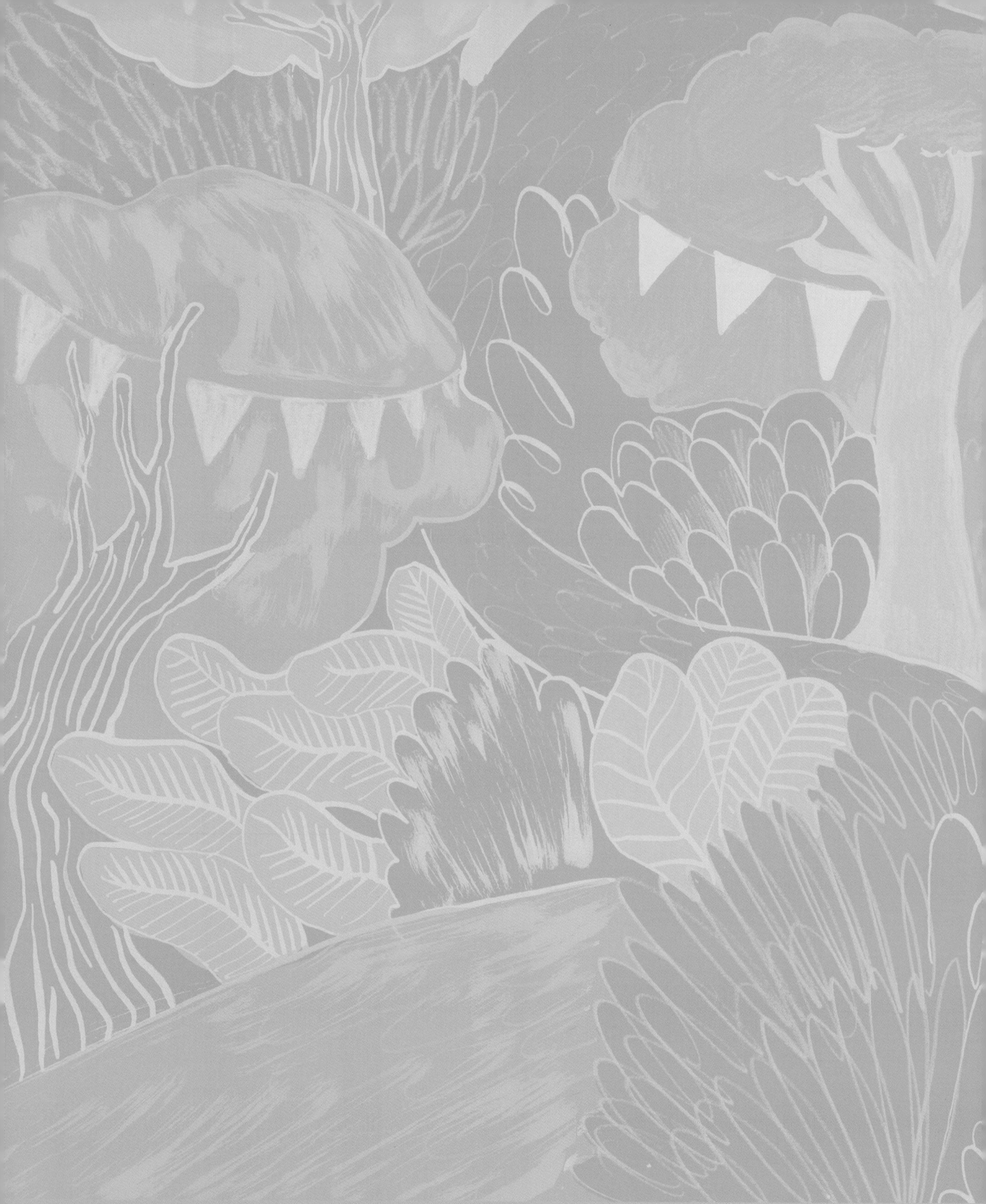

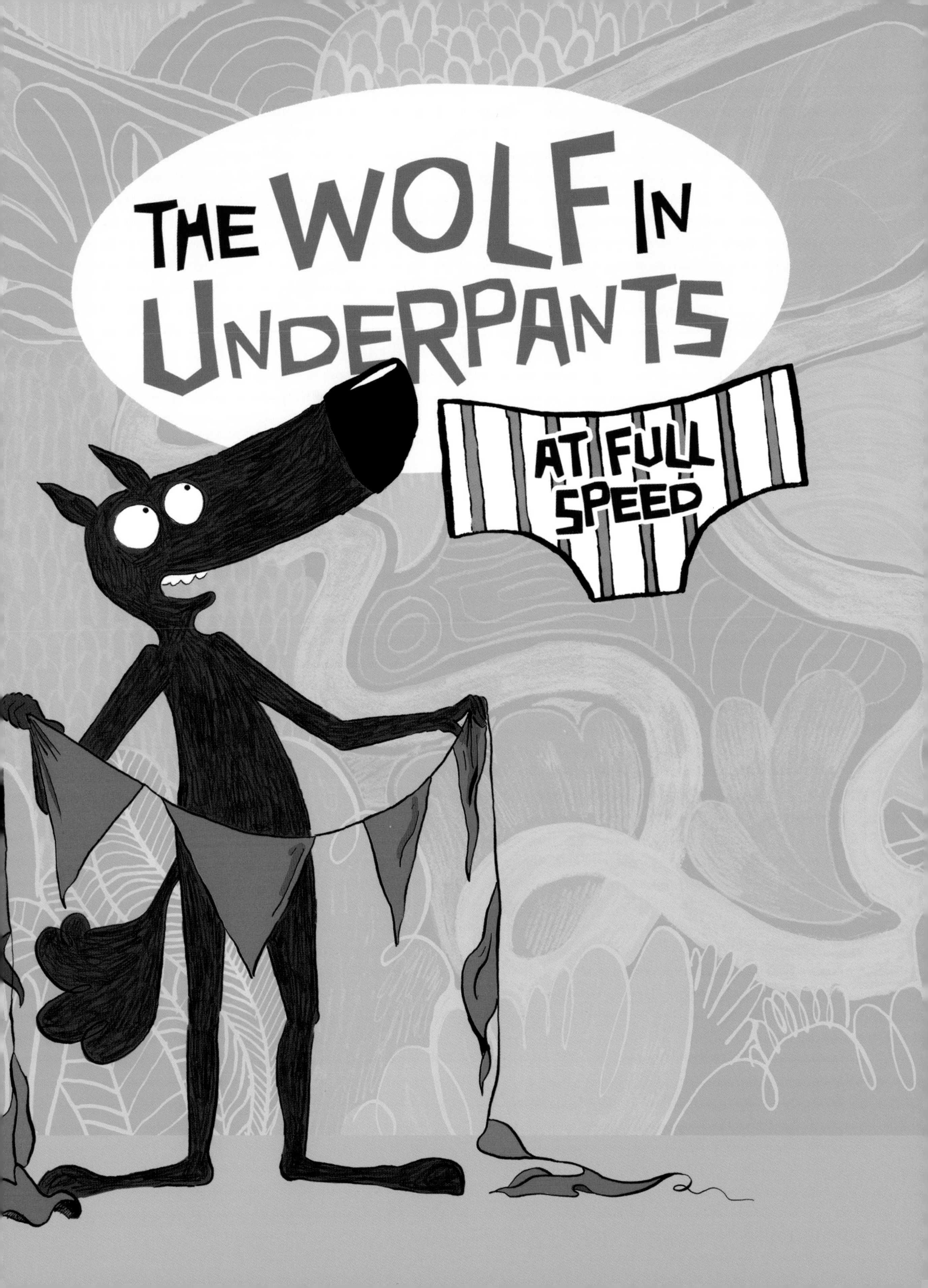
THE WOLF IN UNDERPANTS
AT FULL SPEED

Story by Wilfrid Lupano
Art by Mayana Itoïz
With the friendly artistic participation of Paul Cauuet
Translation by Nathan Sacks

First American edition published in 2021 by Graphic Universe™
Published by arrangement with Mediatoon Licensing - France
Le Loup en slip hip hip!
© Dargaud Benelux (Dargaud-Lombard S.A.) 2018—Lupano, Itoïz, and Cauuet. All rights
reserved. Original artistic director: Philippe Ravon.
www.dargaud.com

English translation copyright © 2021 by Lerner Publishing Group, Inc.

Graphic Universe™ is a trademark of Lerner Publishing Group, Inc.

Graphic Universe™
An imprint of Lerner Publishing Group, Inc.
241 First Avenue North
Minneapolis, MN 55401 USA

For reading levels and more information, look up this title at www.lernerbooks.com.

Main body text set in Stick-A-Round. Typeface provided by Pintassilgoprints.

Library of Congress Cataloging-in-Publication Data

Names: Lupano, Wilfrid, 1971- author. | Itoïz, Mayana, 1978- artist. | Cauuet, Paul, 1980-
    artist. | Sacks, Nathan, translator.
Title: The wolf in underpants at full speed / story by Wilfrid Lupano ; art by Mayana Itoïz,
    with the friendly artistic participation of Paul Cauuet ; translation by Nathan Sacks.
Other titles: Loup en slip hip hip!. English
Description: First American edition. | Minneapolis : Graphic Universe, 2021. | Series: The wolf in
    underpants | Audience: Ages 7-11 | Audience: Grades 2-3 | Summary: "It's race day in the
    forest, but a surly chickadee has ruined the event's posters! When the Wolf learns why the
    little bird feels left out, he hatches a plan to launch it to victory" —Provided by publisher.
Identifiers: LCCN 2020021367 (print) | LCCN 2020021368 (ebook) | ISBN 9781728412979
    (library binding) | ISBN 9781728420233 (paperback) | ISBN 9781728417530 (ebook)
Subjects: LCSH: Graphic novels. | CYAC: Graphic novels. | Wolves—Fiction. | Forest animals—
    Fiction.
Classification: LCC PZ7.7.L86 Wp 2021 (print) | LCC PZ7.7.L86 (ebook) | DDC 741.5/973—dc23

LC record available at https://lccn.loc.gov/2020021367
LC ebook record available at https://lccn.loc.gov/2020021368

Manufactured in the United States of America
1-48541-49042-9/25/2020

THE WOLF IN UNDERPANTS

AT FULL SPEED

Wilfrid Lupano

Mayana Itoïz
and
Paul Cauuet

Graphic Universe™ • Minneapolis

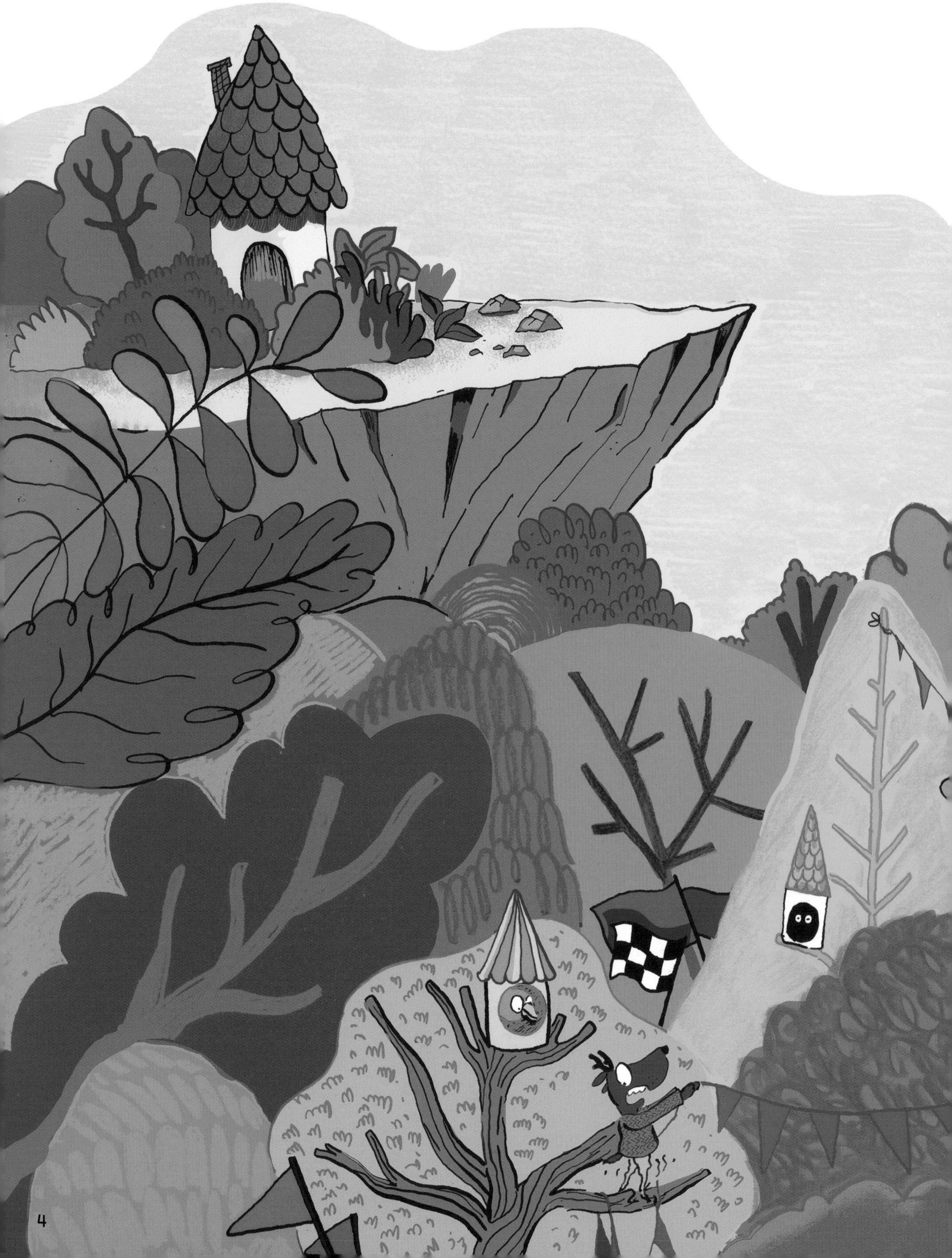

IT'S AN EXCITING DAY IN THE FOREST! EVERYONE'S TAKING OUT PENNANTS AND POM-POMS, BECAUSE TODAY IS . . .

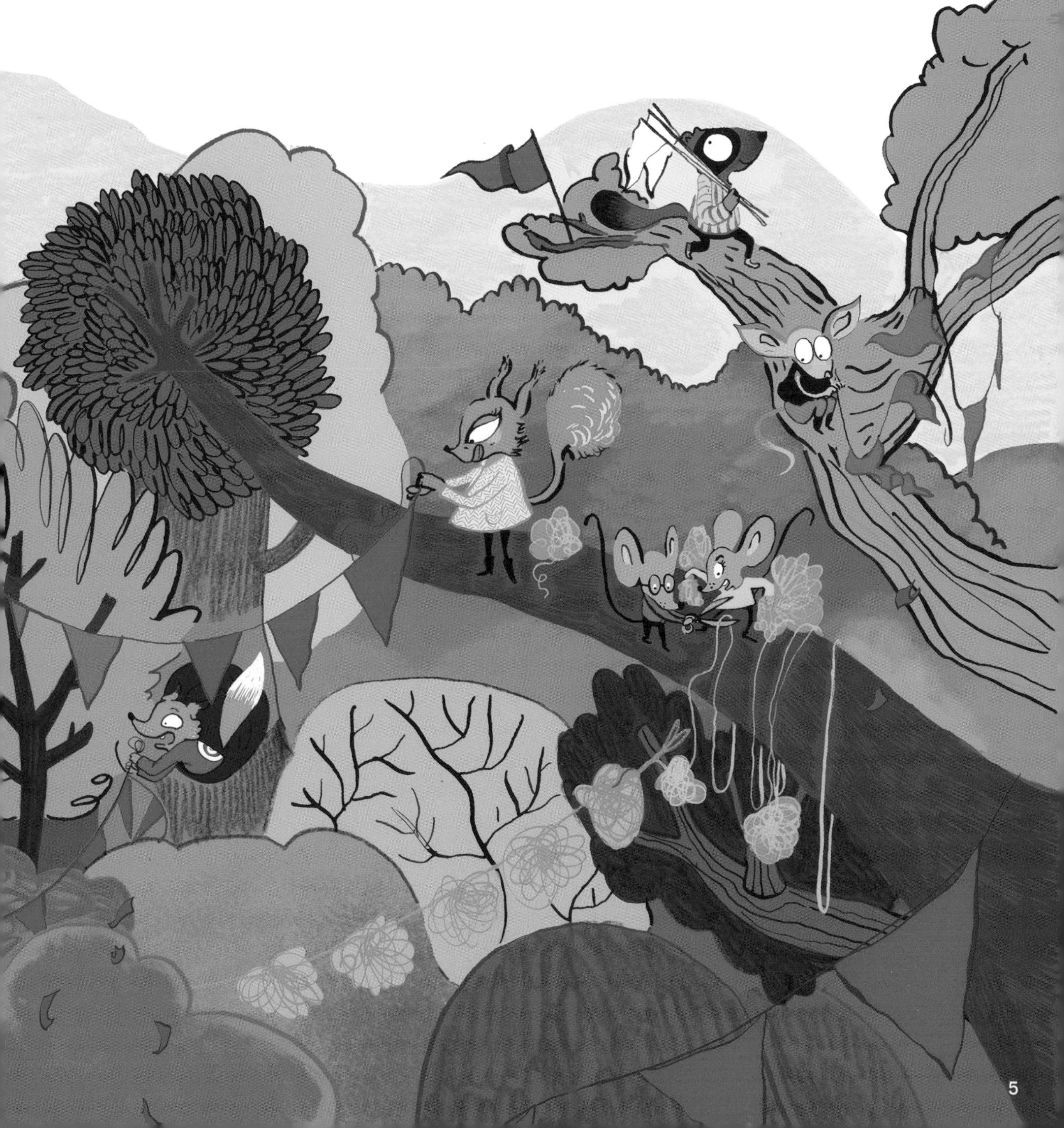

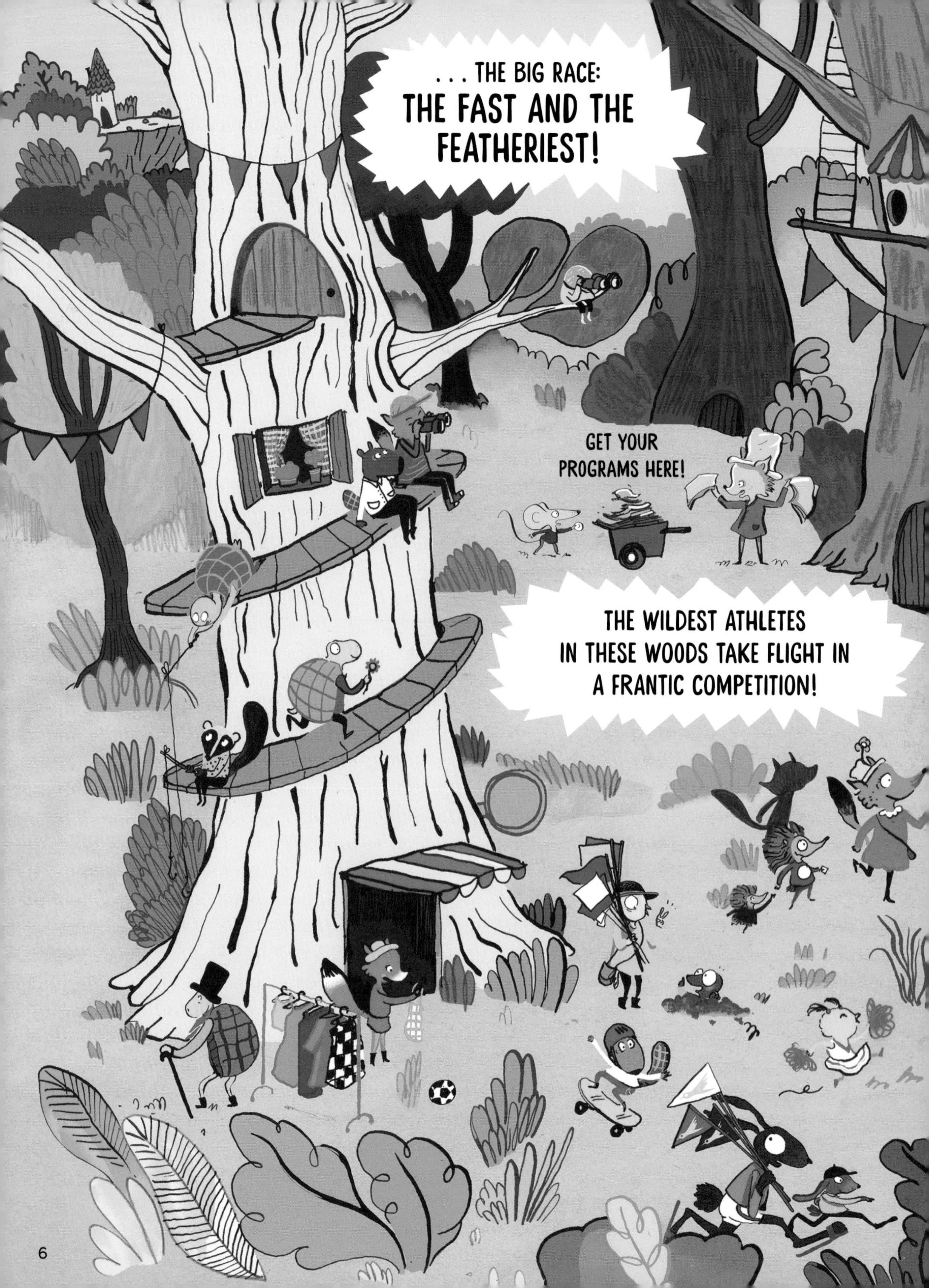
. . . THE BIG RACE:
THE FAST AND THE FEATHERIEST!
GET YOUR PROGRAMS HERE!
THE WILDEST ATHLETES IN THESE WOODS TAKE FLIGHT IN A FRANTIC COMPETITION!

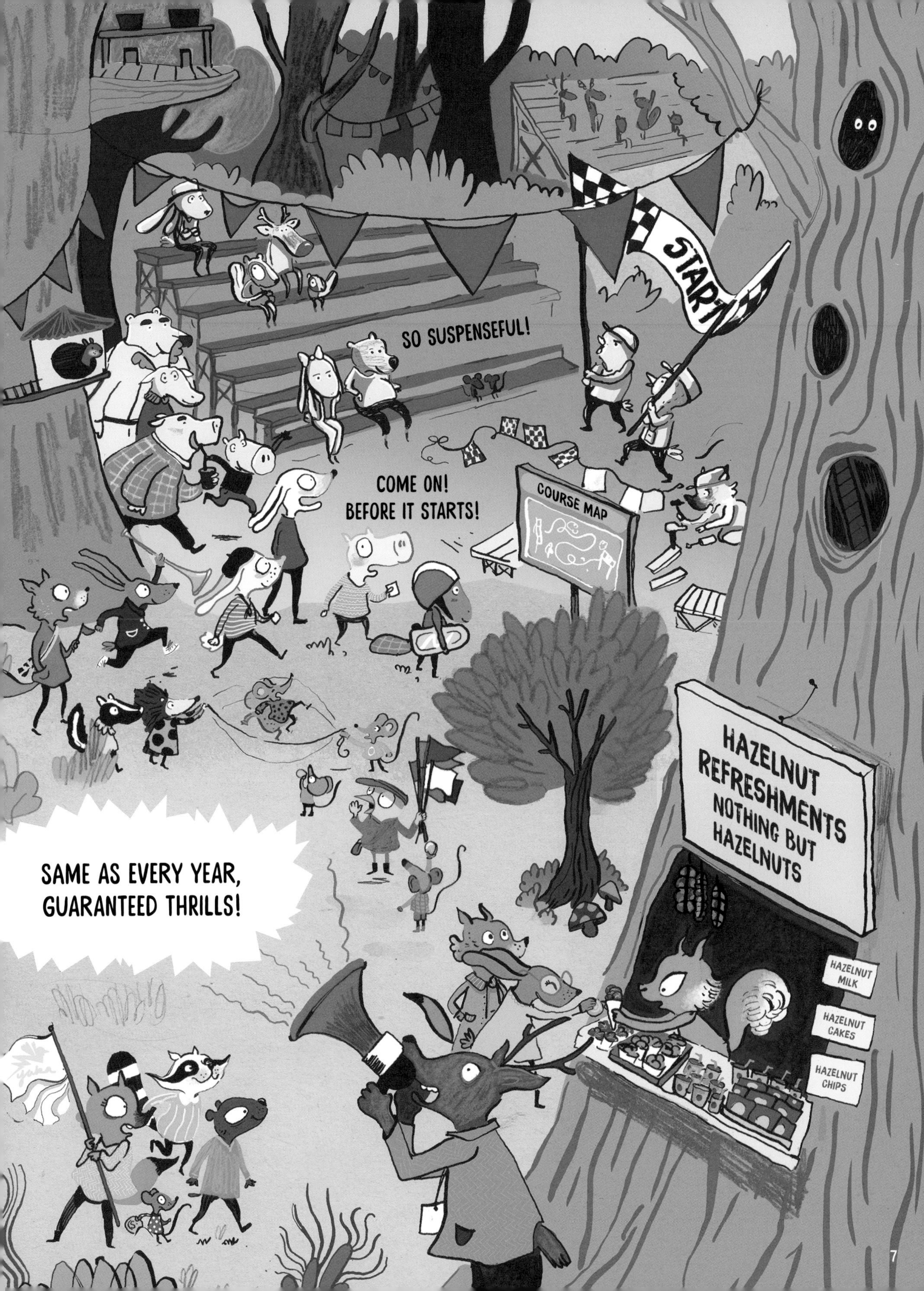

START
SO SUSPENSEFUL!
COME ON!
BEFORE IT STARTS!
COURSE MAP
HAZELNUT
REFRESHMENTS
NOTHING BUT
HAZELNUTS
SAME AS EVERY YEAR,
GUARANTEED THRILLS!
HAZELNUT MILK
HAZELNUT CAKES
HAZELNUT CHIPS

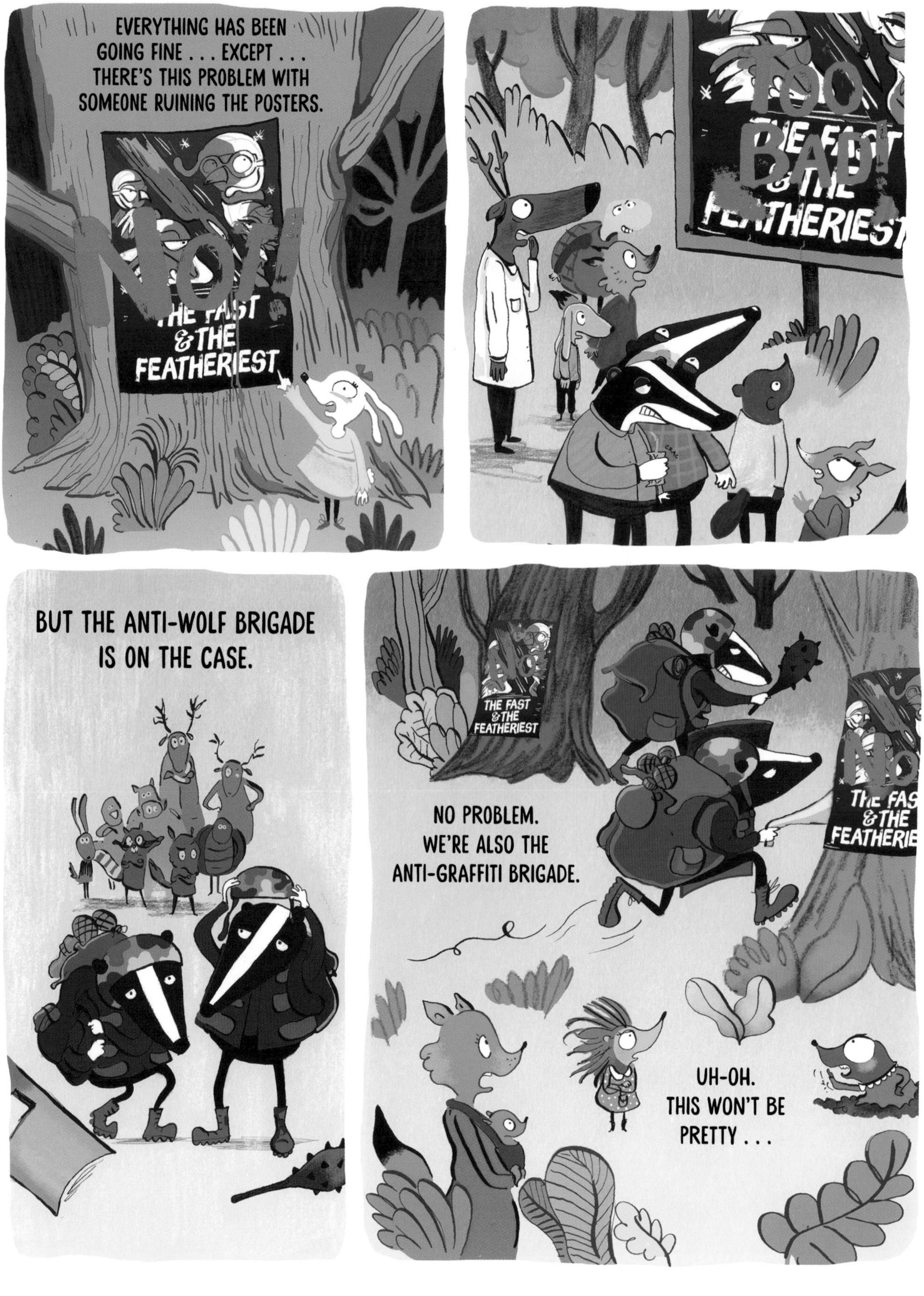
EVERYTHING HAS BEEN GOING FINE . . . EXCEPT . . . THERE'S THIS PROBLEM WITH SOMEONE RUINING THE POSTERS.
NO!
THE FAST & THE FEATHERIEST
TOO BAD!
THE FAST & THE FEATHERIEST
BUT THE ANTI-WOLF BRIGADE IS ON THE CASE.
THE FAST & THE FEATHERIEST
NO PROBLEM. WE'RE ALSO THE ANTI-GRAFFITI BRIGADE.
UH-OH. THIS WON'T BE PRETTY . . .

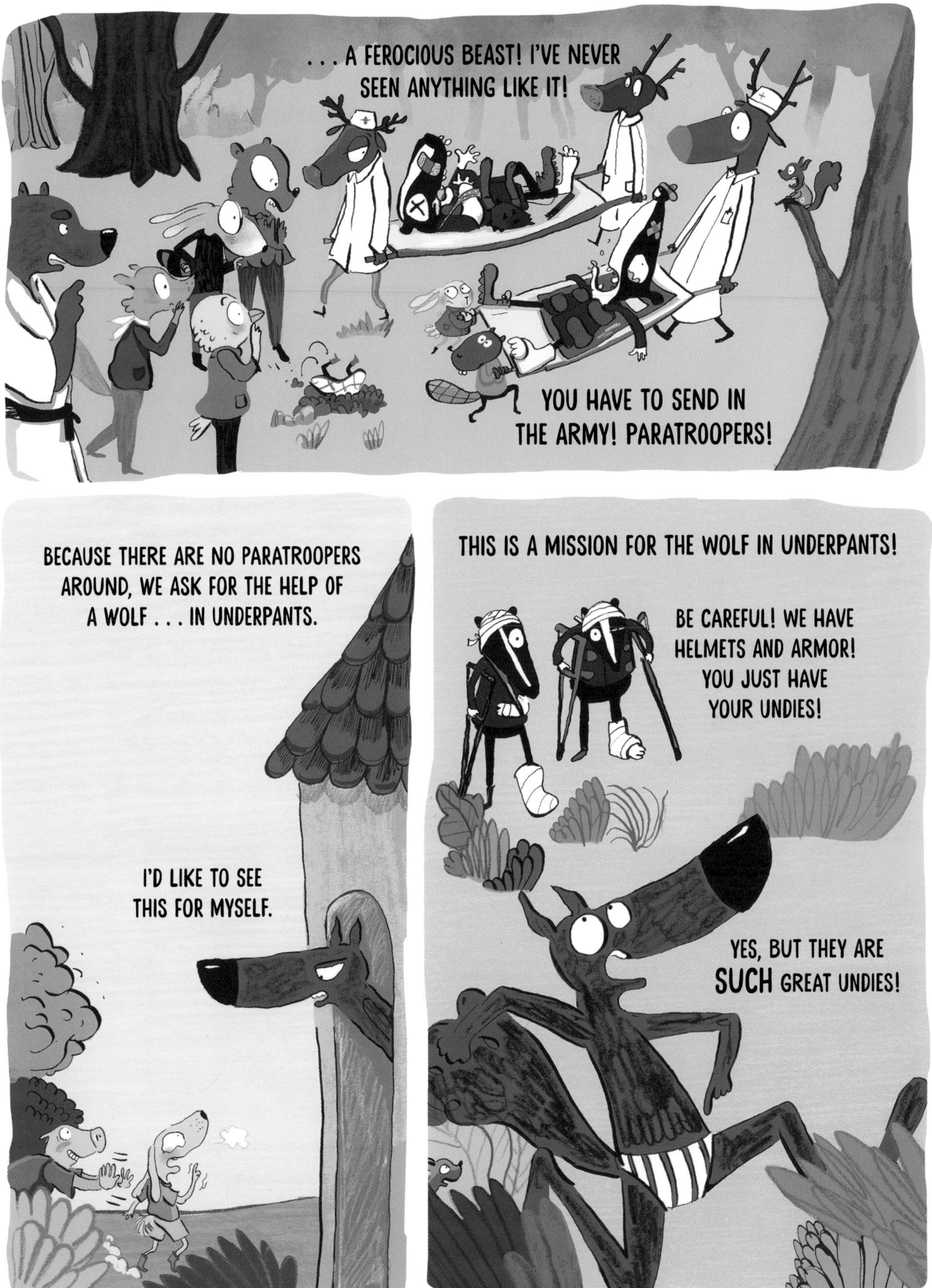
. . . A FEROCIOUS BEAST! I'VE NEVER SEEN ANYTHING LIKE IT!
YOU HAVE TO SEND IN THE ARMY! PARATROOPERS!
BECAUSE THERE ARE NO PARATROOPERS AROUND, WE ASK FOR THE HELP OF A WOLF . . . IN UNDERPANTS.
I'D LIKE TO SEE THIS FOR MYSELF.
THIS IS A MISSION FOR THE WOLF IN UNDERPANTS!
BE CAREFUL! WE HAVE HELMETS AND ARMOR! YOU JUST HAVE YOUR UNDIES!
YES, BUT THEY ARE **SUCH** GREAT UNDIES!

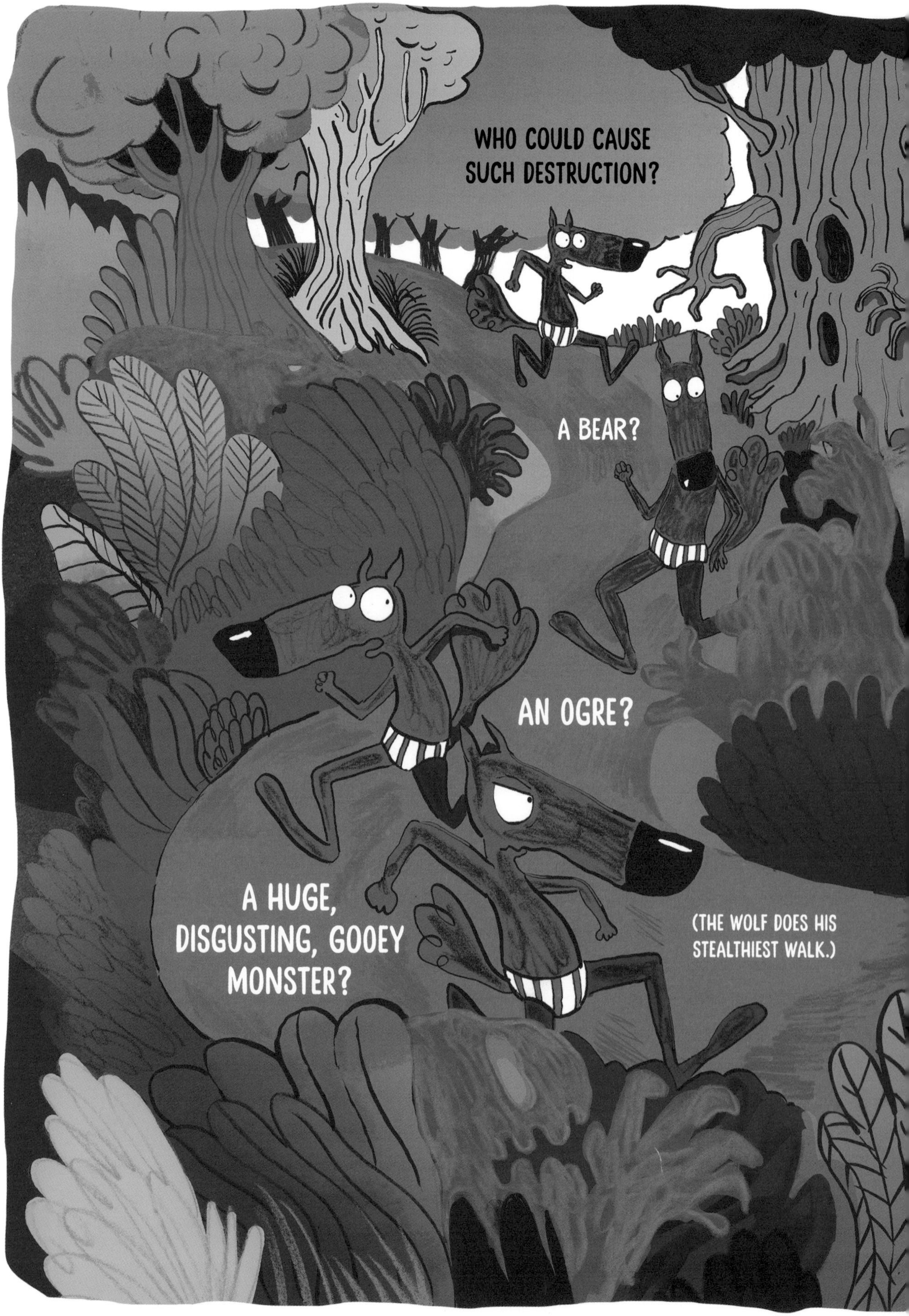
WHO COULD CAUSE SUCH DESTRUCTION?
A BEAR?
AN OGRE?
A HUGE, DISGUSTING, GOOEY MONSTER?
(THE WOLF DOES HIS STEALTHIEST WALK.)

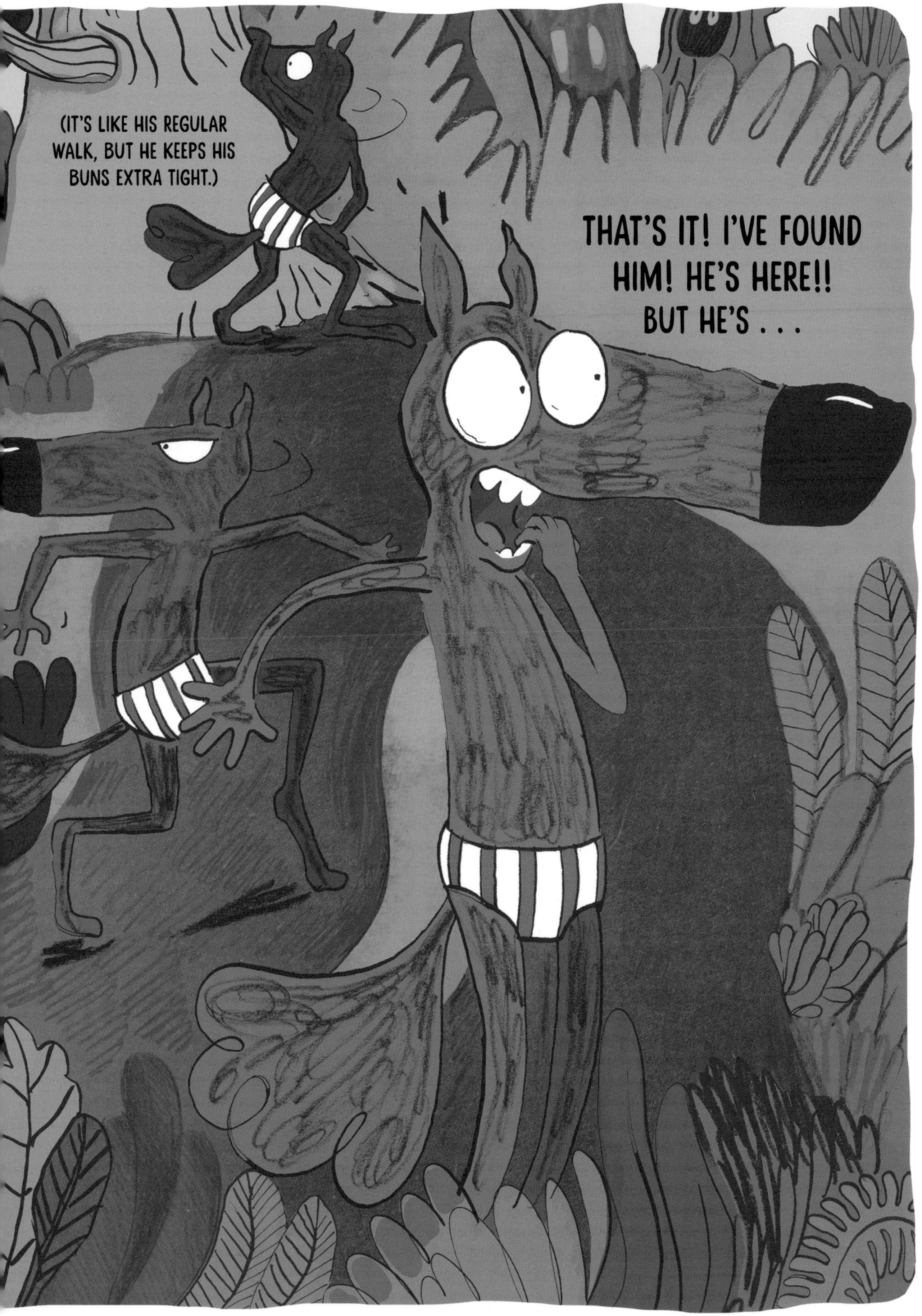
(IT'S LIKE HIS REGULAR WALK, BUT HE KEEPS HIS BUNS EXTRA TIGHT.)
THAT'S IT! I'VE FOUND HIM! HE'S HERE!! BUT HE'S . . .

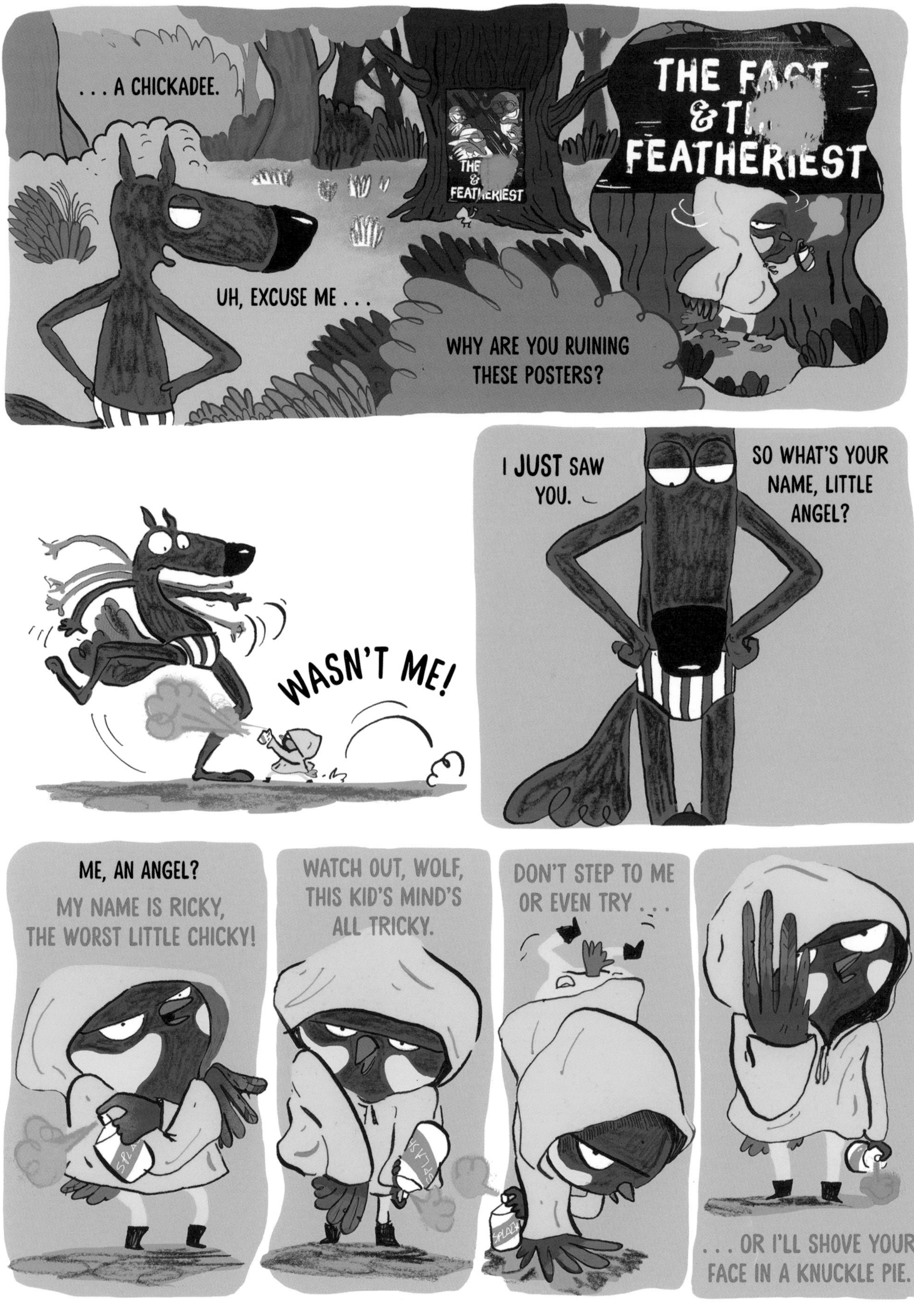

. . . A CHICKADEE.
THE FAST & THE FEATHERIEST
THE & FEATHERIEST
UH, EXCUSE ME . . .
WHY ARE YOU RUINING THESE POSTERS?
WASN'T ME!
I JUST SAW YOU.
SO WHAT'S YOUR NAME, LITTLE ANGEL?
ME, AN ANGEL?
MY NAME IS RICKY, THE WORST LITTLE CHICKY!
WATCH OUT, WOLF, THIS KID'S MIND'S ALL TRICKY.
DON'T STEP TO ME OR EVEN TRY . . .
. . . OR I'LL SHOVE YOUR FACE IN A KNUCKLE PIE.

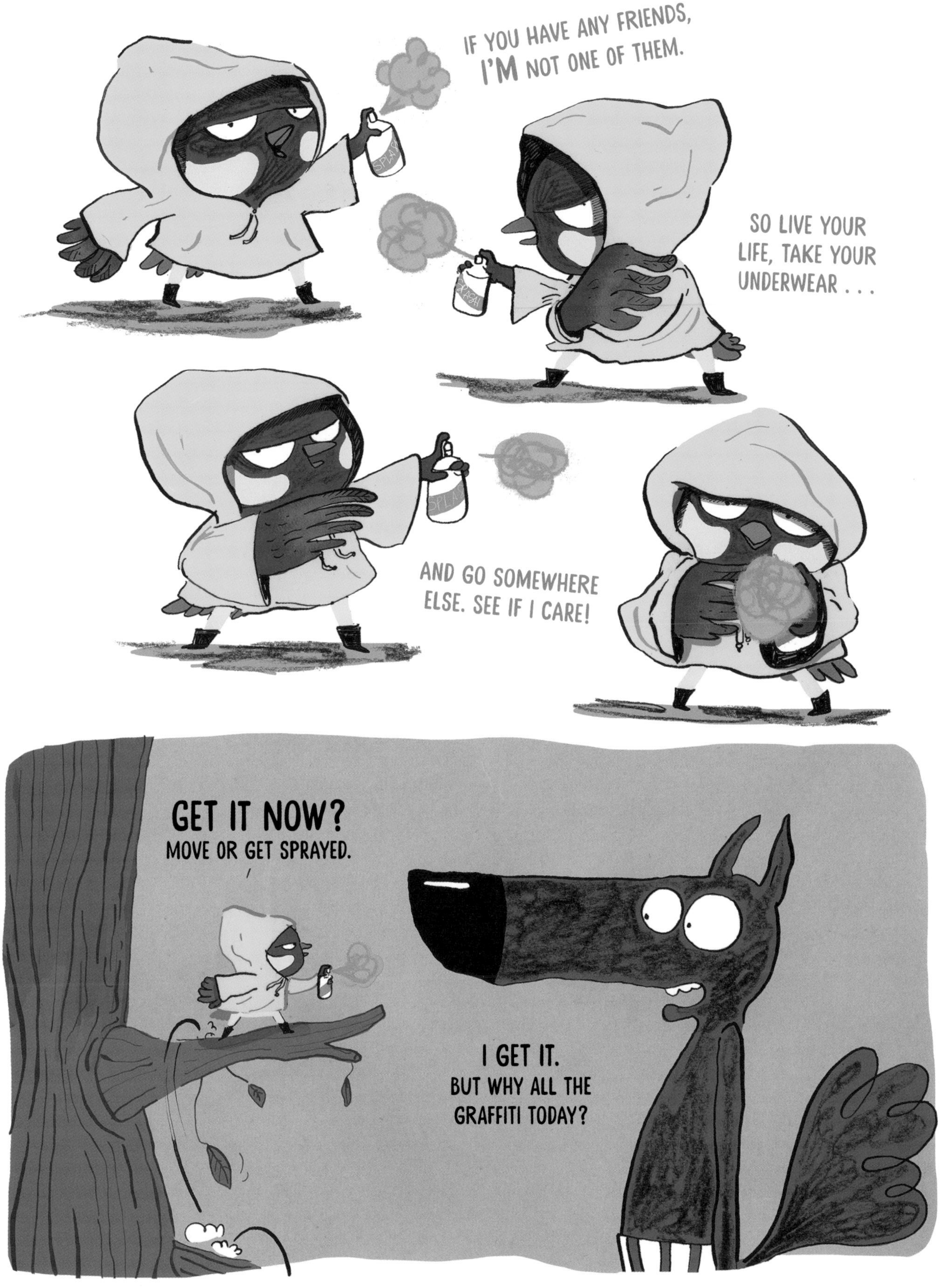
IF YOU HAVE ANY FRIENDS,
I'M NOT ONE OF THEM.
SO LIVE YOUR LIFE, TAKE YOUR UNDERWEAR . . .
AND GO SOMEWHERE ELSE. SEE IF I CARE!
GET IT NOW?
MOVE OR GET SPRAYED.
I GET IT.
BUT WHY ALL THE GRAFFITI TODAY?

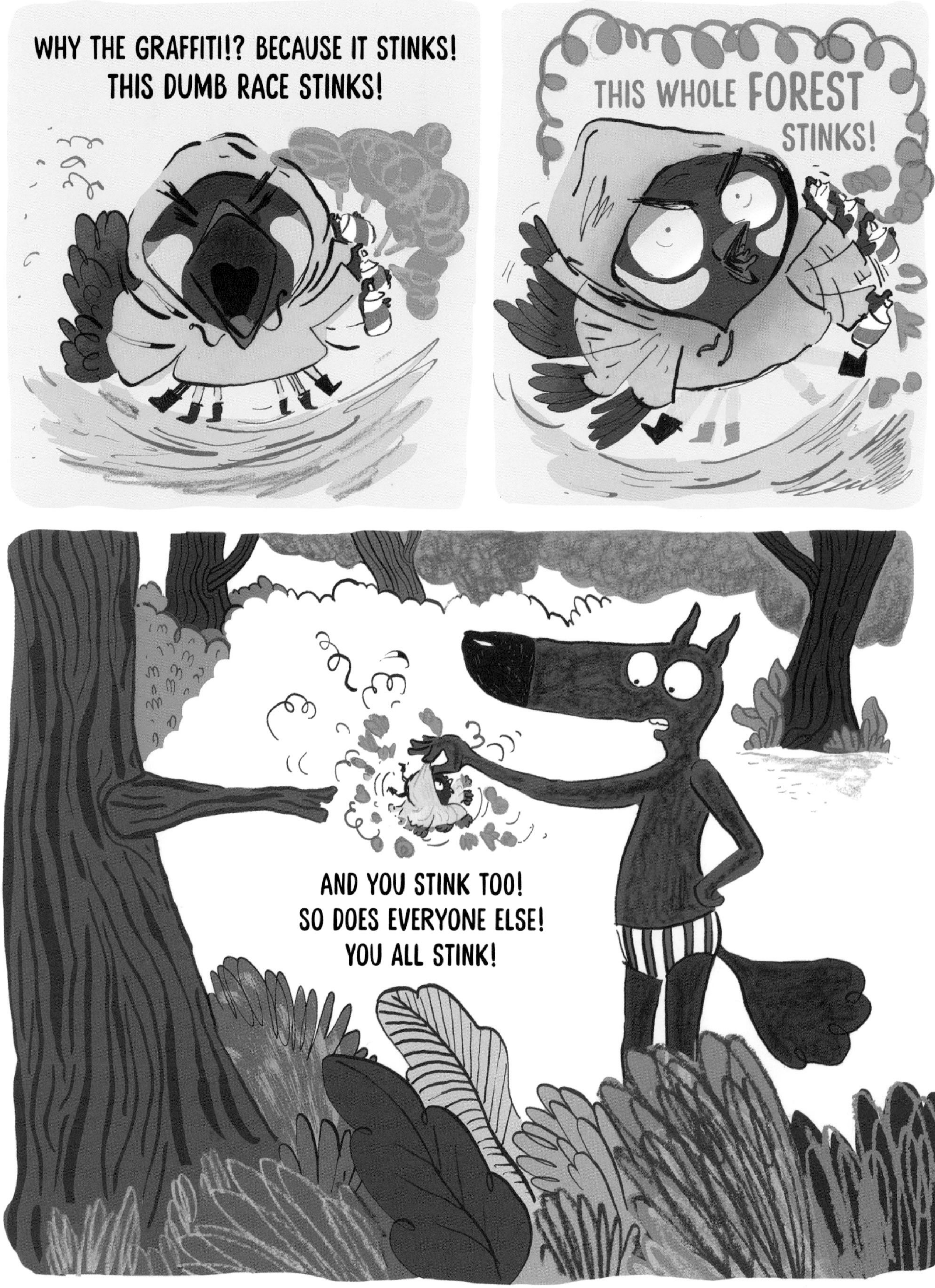
WHY THE GRAFFITI!? BECAUSE IT STINKS! THIS DUMB RACE STINKS!
THIS WHOLE FOREST STINKS!
AND YOU STINK TOO! SO DOES EVERYONE ELSE! YOU ALL STINK!

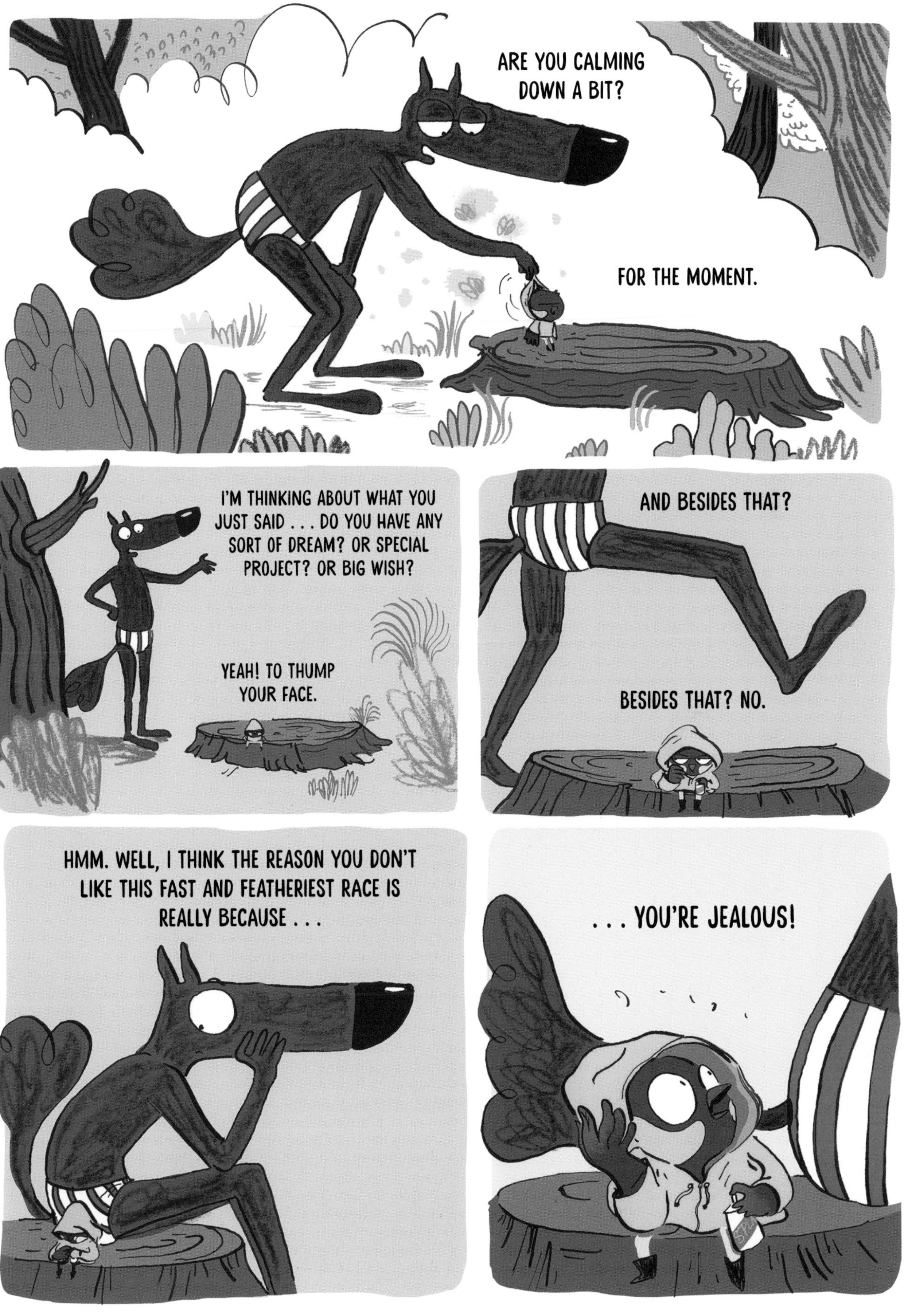
ARE YOU CALMING DOWN A BIT?
FOR THE MOMENT.
I'M THINKING ABOUT WHAT YOU JUST SAID . . . DO YOU HAVE ANY SORT OF DREAM? OR SPECIAL PROJECT? OR BIG WISH?
YEAH! TO THUMP YOUR FACE.
AND BESIDES THAT?
BESIDES THAT? NO.
HMM. WELL, I THINK THE REASON YOU DON'T LIKE THIS FAST AND FEATHERIEST RACE IS REALLY BECAUSE . . .
. . . YOU'RE JEALOUS!

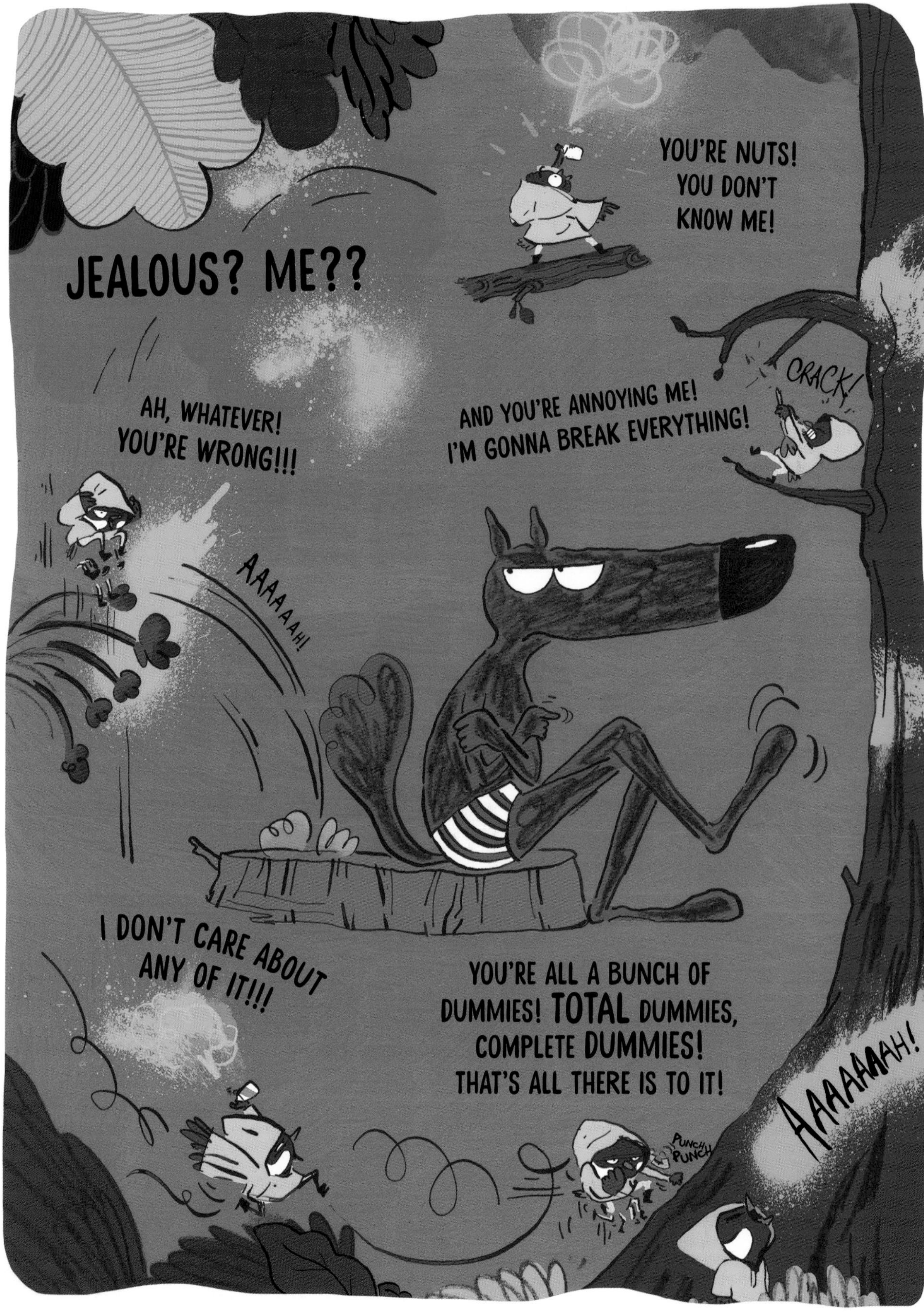

JEALOUS? ME??
YOU'RE NUTS! YOU DON'T KNOW ME!
AH, WHATEVER! YOU'RE WRONG!!!
AND YOU'RE ANNOYING ME! I'M GONNA BREAK EVERYTHING!
CRACK!
AAAAAAAH!
I DON'T CARE ABOUT ANY OF IT!!!
YOU'RE ALL A BUNCH OF DUMMIES! TOTAL DUMMIES, COMPLETE DUMMIES! THAT'S ALL THERE IS TO IT!
AAAAAAAH!
PUNCH PUNCH

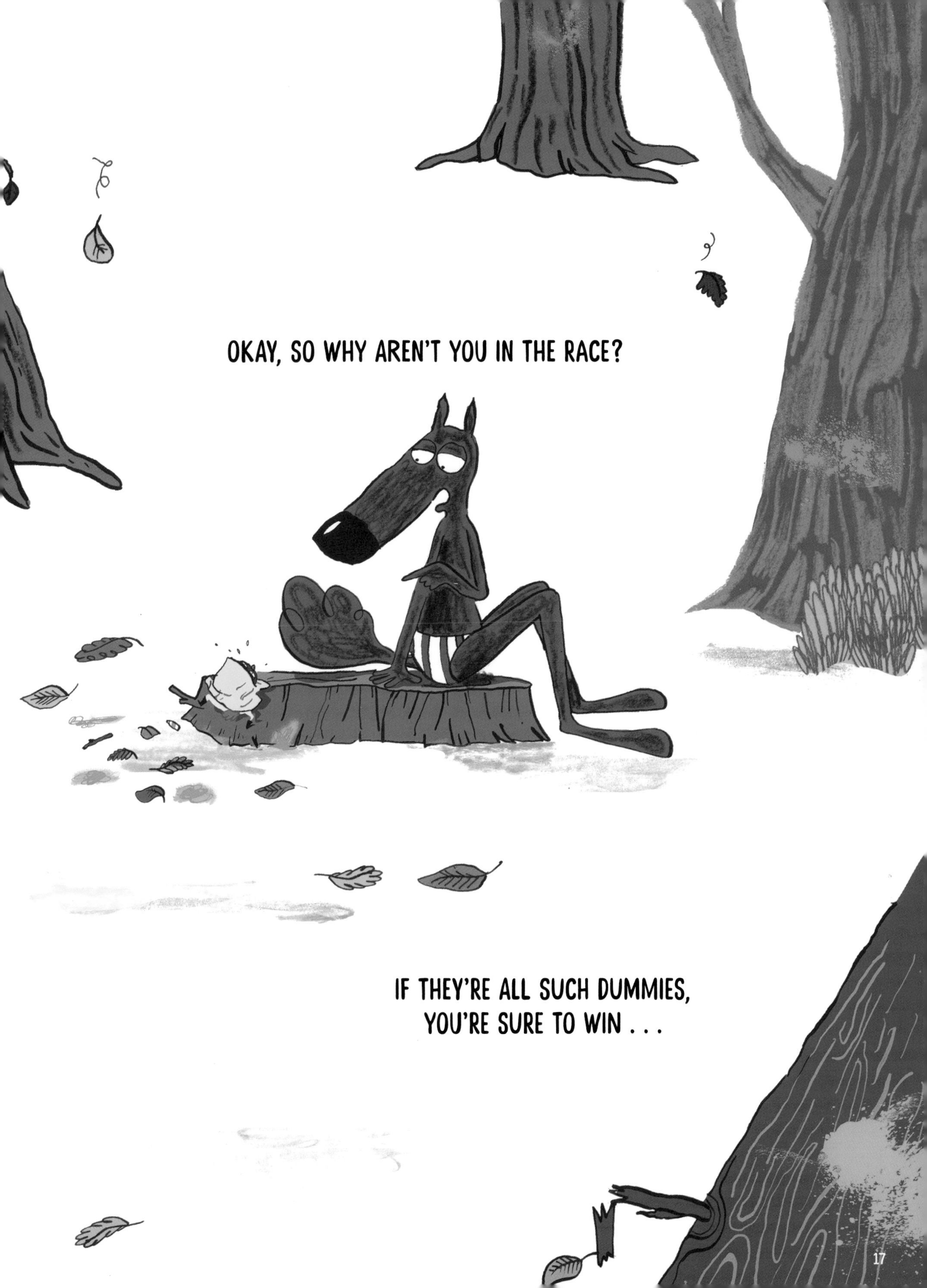
OKAY, SO WHY AREN'T YOU IN THE RACE?
IF THEY'RE ALL SUCH DUMMIES, YOU'RE SURE TO WIN . . .

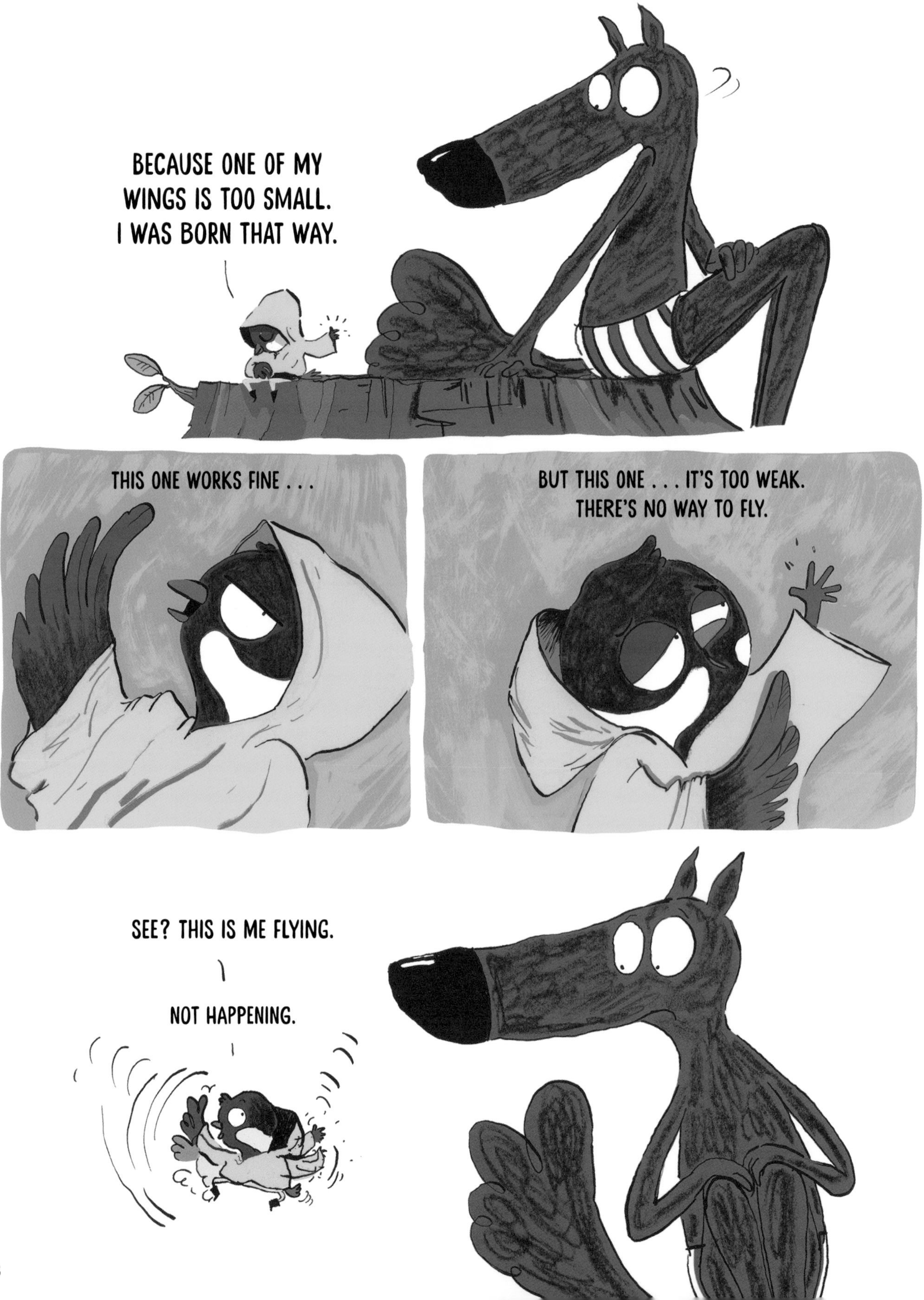
BECAUSE ONE OF MY WINGS IS TOO SMALL. I WAS BORN THAT WAY.
THIS ONE WORKS FINE . . .
BUT THIS ONE . . . IT'S TOO WEAK. THERE'S NO WAY TO FLY.
SEE? THIS IS ME FLYING.
NOT HAPPENING.

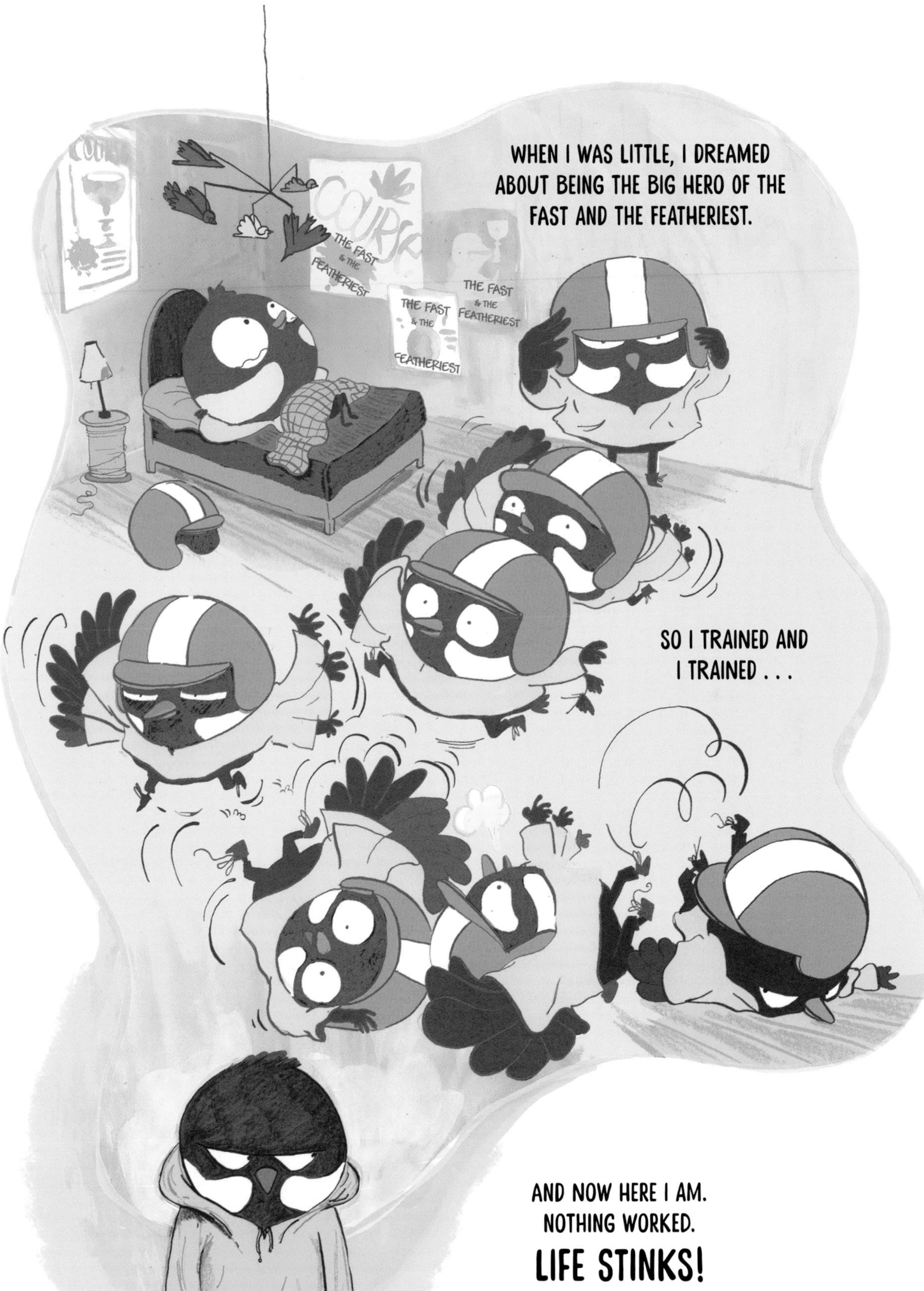
WHEN I WAS LITTLE, I DREAMED ABOUT BEING THE BIG HERO OF THE FAST AND THE FEATHERIEST.
THE FAST & THE FEATHERIEST
THE FAST & THE FEATHERIEST
THE FAST & THE FEATHERIEST
SO I TRAINED AND I TRAINED . . .
AND NOW HERE I AM.
NOTHING WORKED.
LIFE STINKS!

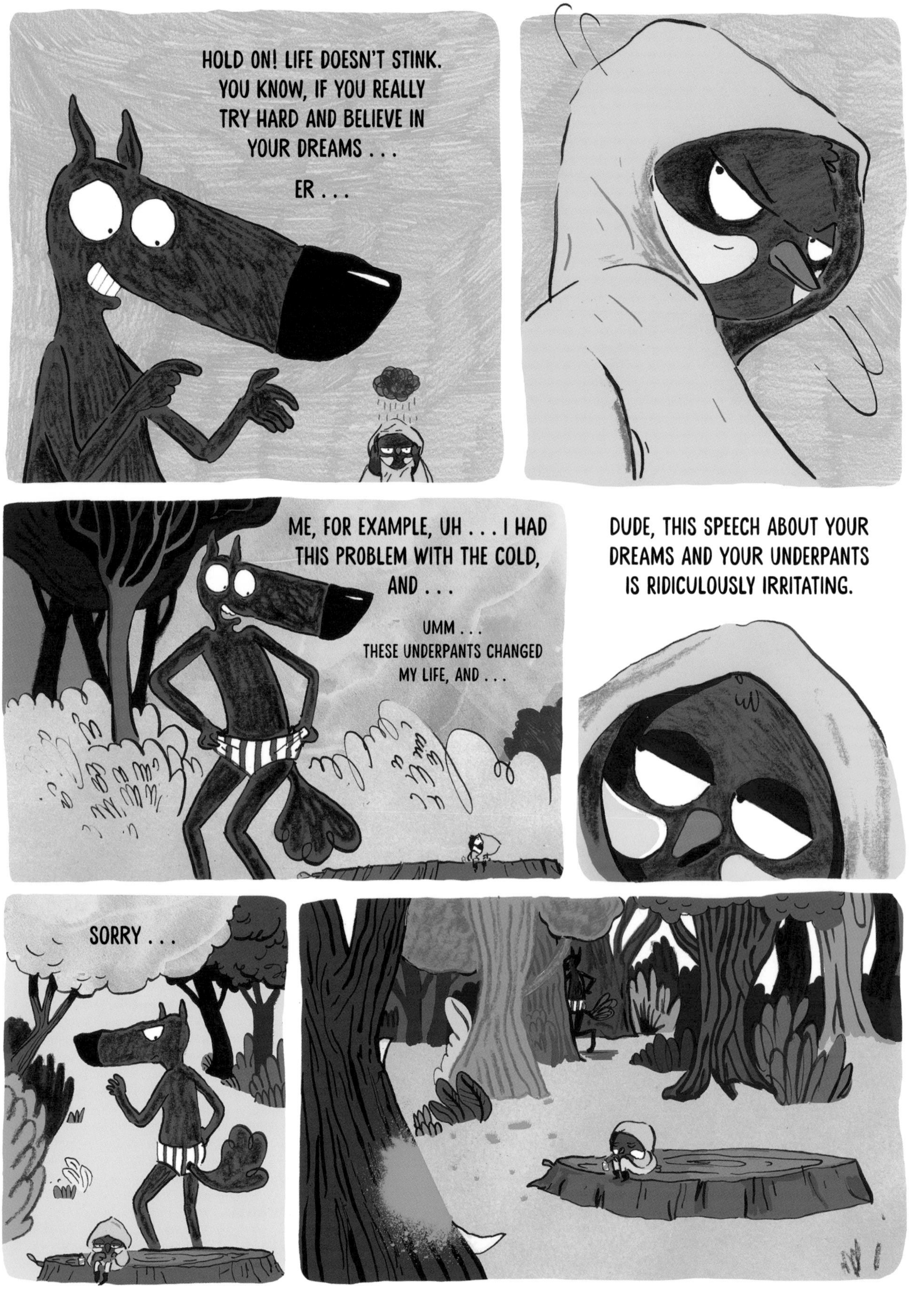
HOLD ON! LIFE DOESN'T STINK. YOU KNOW, IF YOU REALLY TRY HARD AND BELIEVE IN YOUR DREAMS . . .
ER . . .
ME, FOR EXAMPLE, UH . . . I HAD THIS PROBLEM WITH THE COLD, AND . . .
UMM . . . THESE UNDERPANTS CHANGED MY LIFE, AND . . .
DUDE, THIS SPEECH ABOUT YOUR DREAMS AND YOUR UNDERPANTS IS RIDICULOUSLY IRRITATING.
SORRY . . .

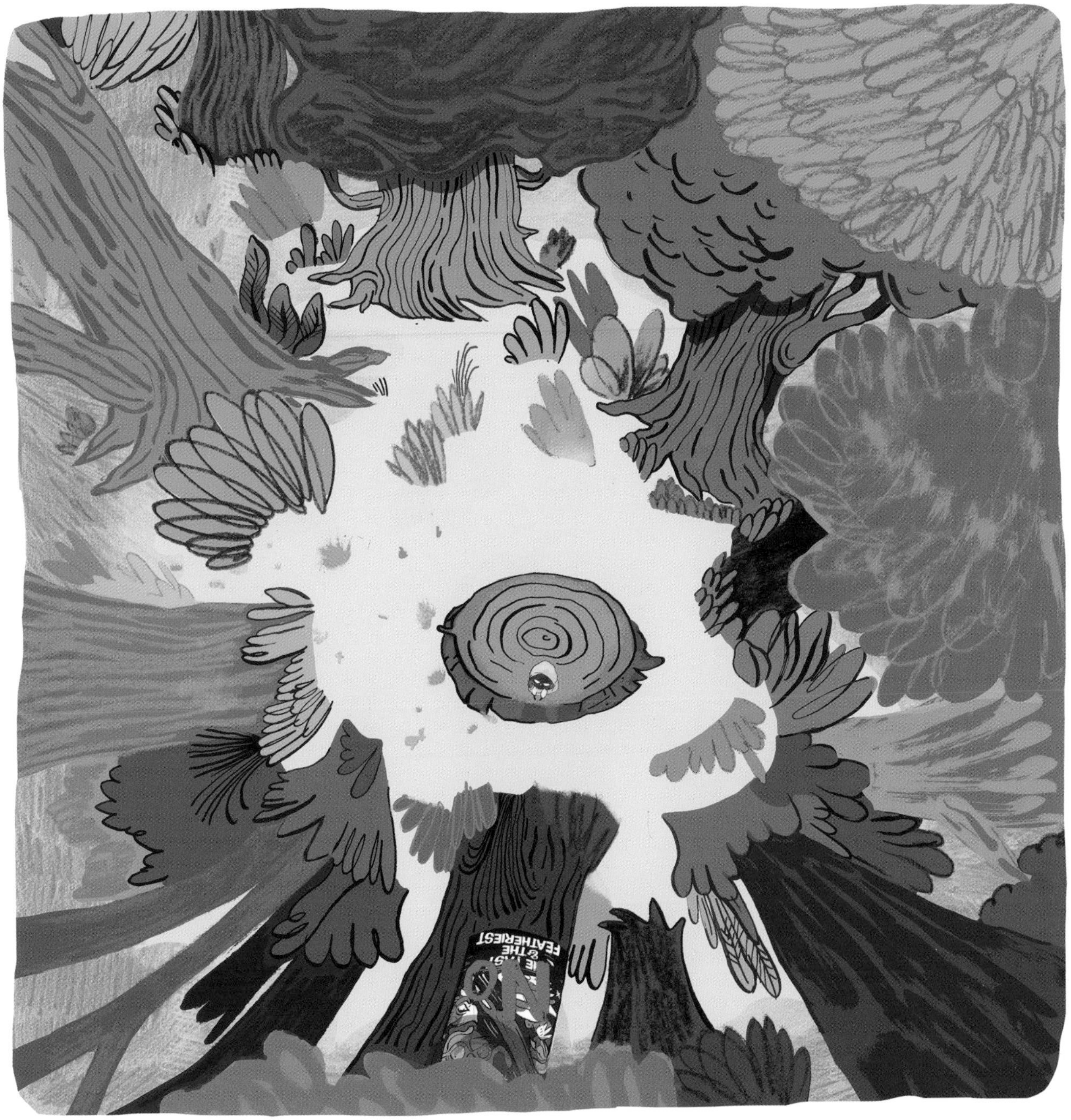

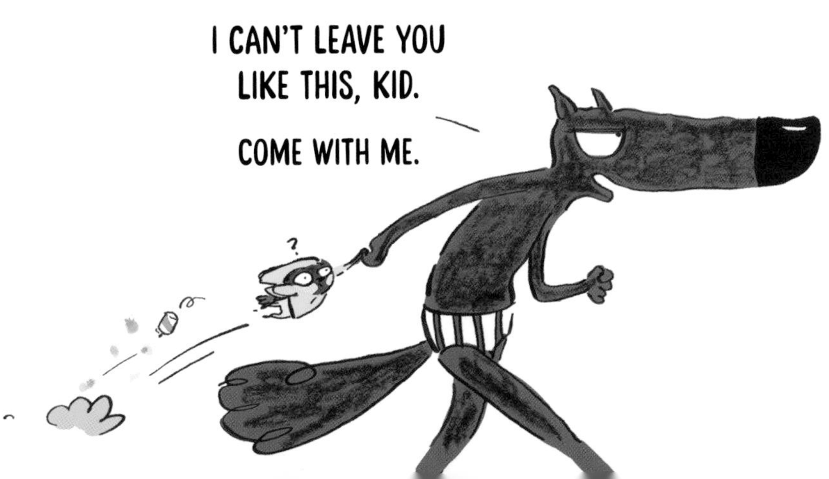
I CAN'T LEAVE YOU LIKE THIS, KID.
COME WITH ME.

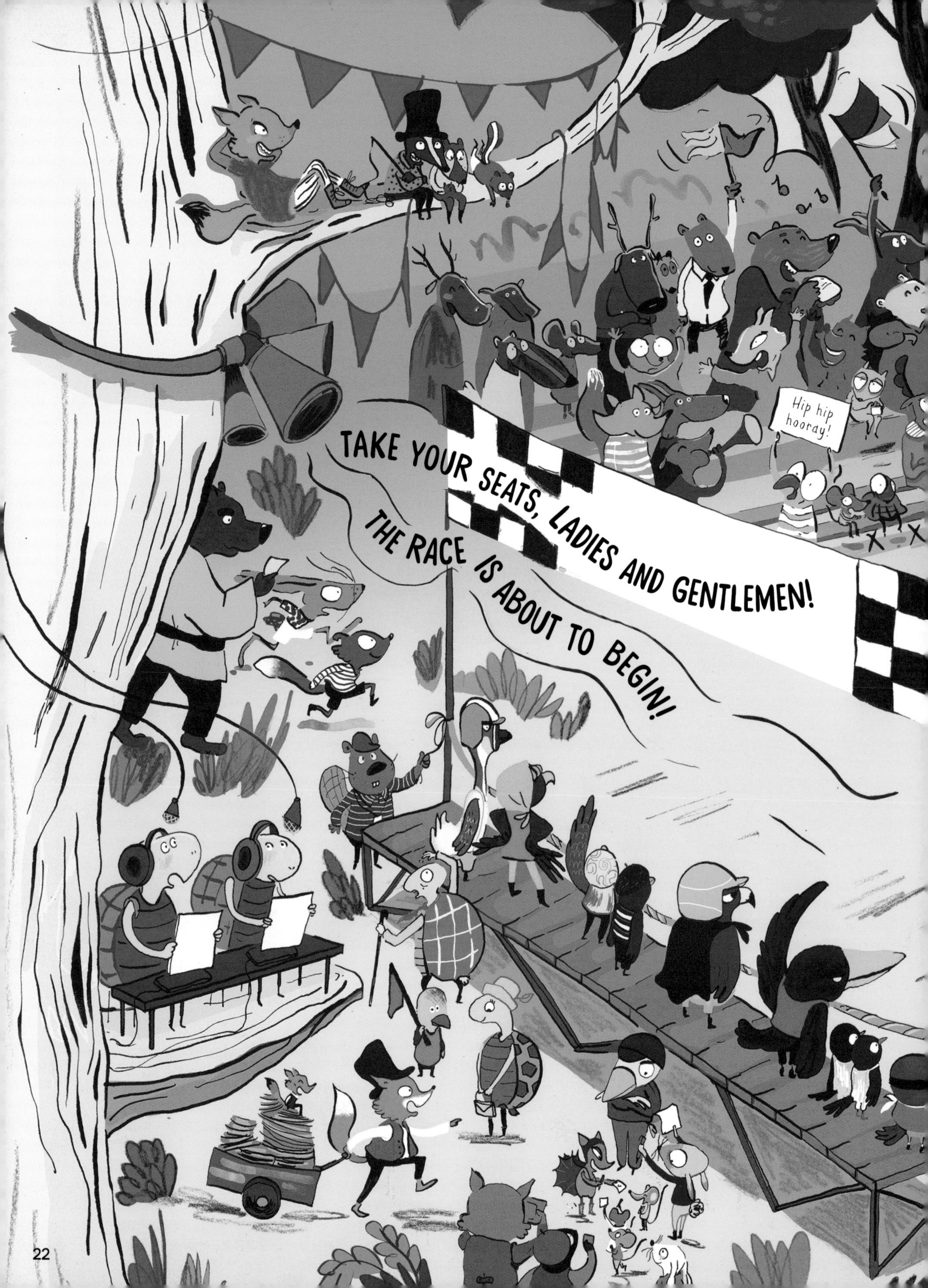
TAKE YOUR SEATS, LADIES AND GENTLEMEN!
THE RACE IS ABOUT TO BEGIN!
Hip hip hooray!

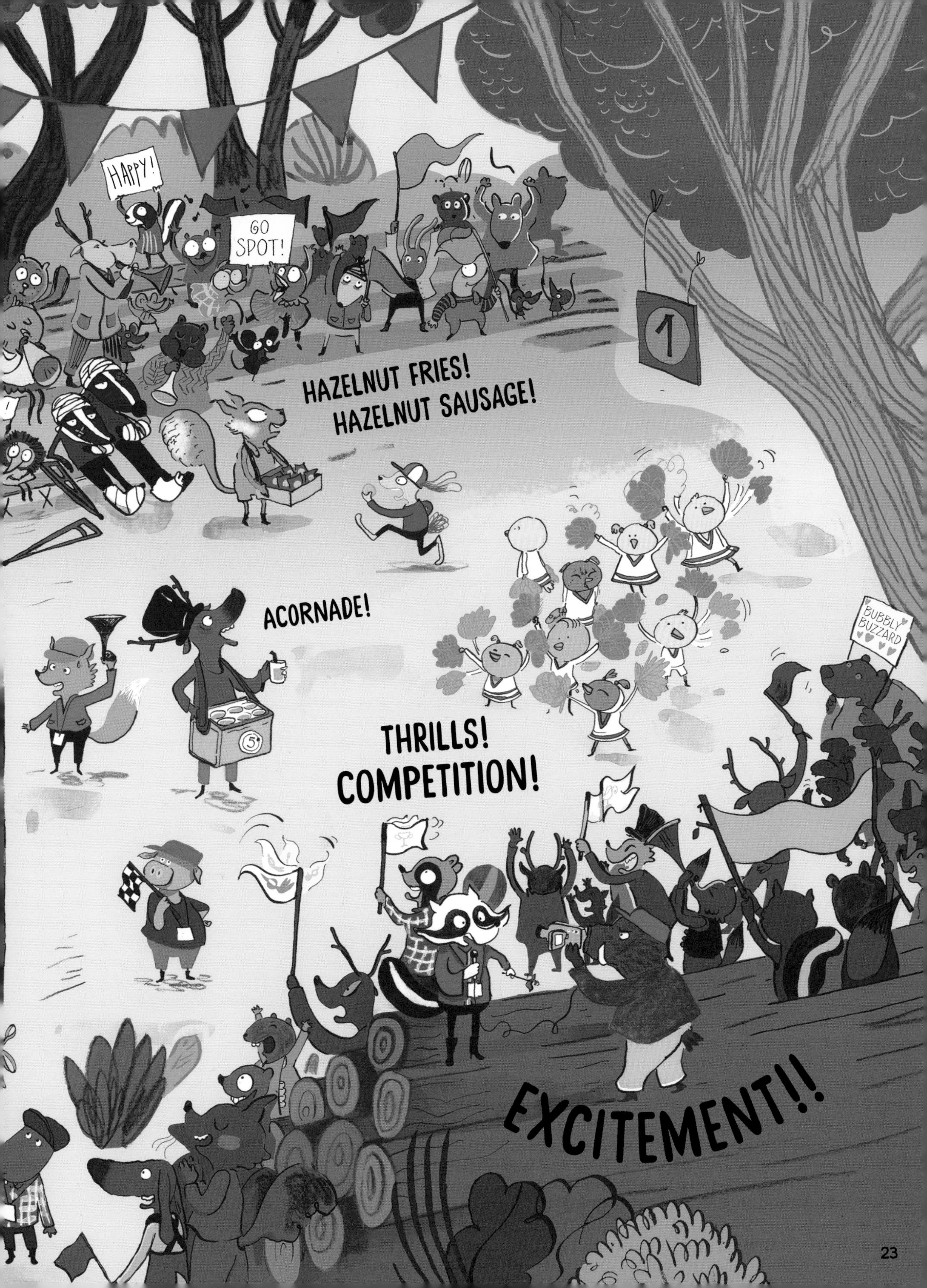
HAPPY!
GO SPOT!
1
HAZELNUT FRIES!
HAZELNUT SAUSAGE!
ACORNADE!
BUBBLY BUZZARD
THRILLS!
COMPETITION!
EXCITEMENT!!

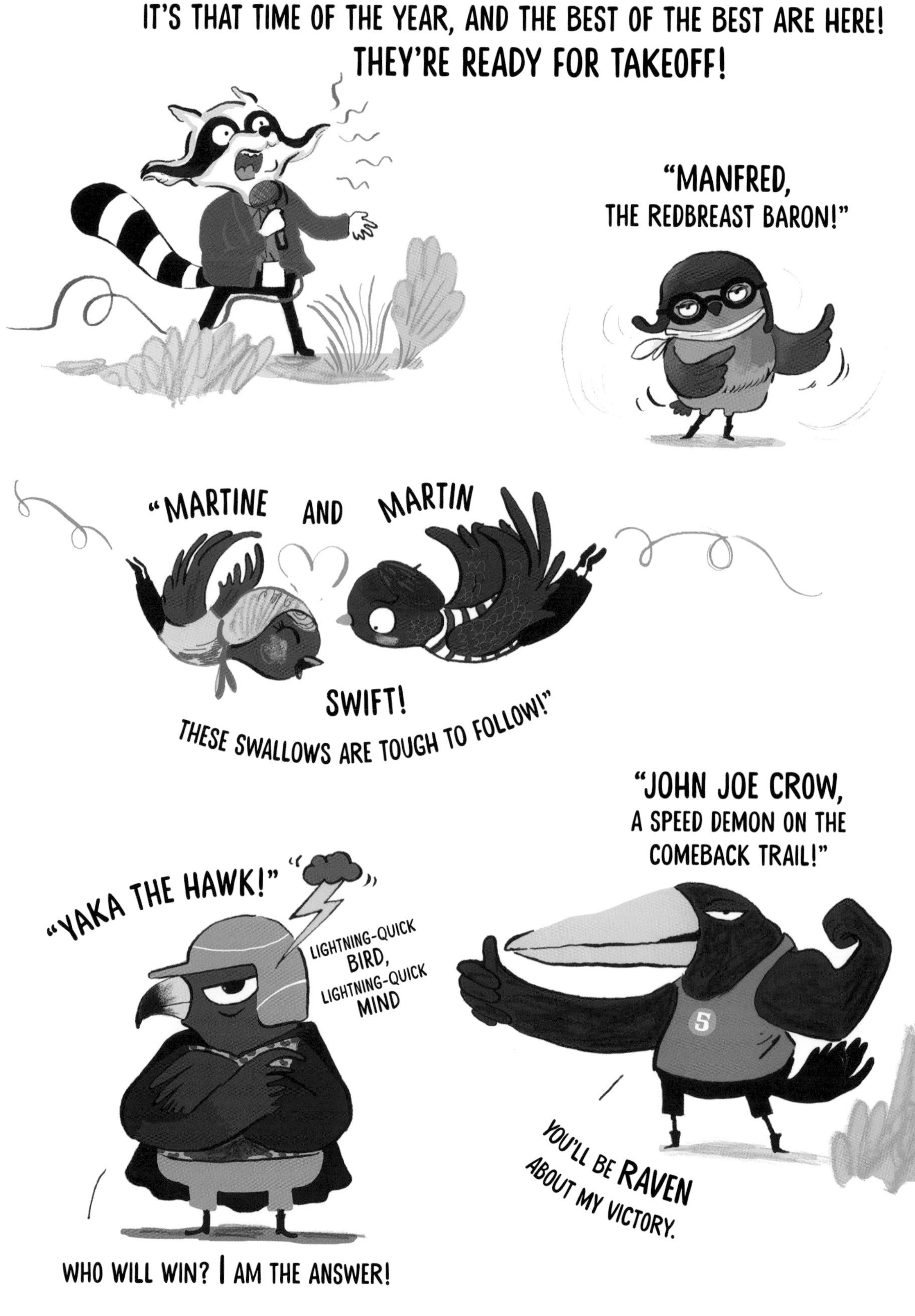
IT'S THAT TIME OF THE YEAR, AND THE BEST OF THE BEST ARE HERE!
THEY'RE READY FOR TAKEOFF!
"MANFRED, THE REDBREAST BARON!"
"MARTINE AND MARTIN
SWIFT!
THESE SWALLOWS ARE TOUGH TO FOLLOW!"
"JOHN JOE CROW, A SPEED DEMON ON THE COMEBACK TRAIL!"
"YAKA THE HAWK!"
LIGHTNING-QUICK BIRD, LIGHTNING-QUICK MIND
YOU'LL BE RAVEN ABOUT MY VICTORY.
WHO WILL WIN? I AM THE ANSWER!

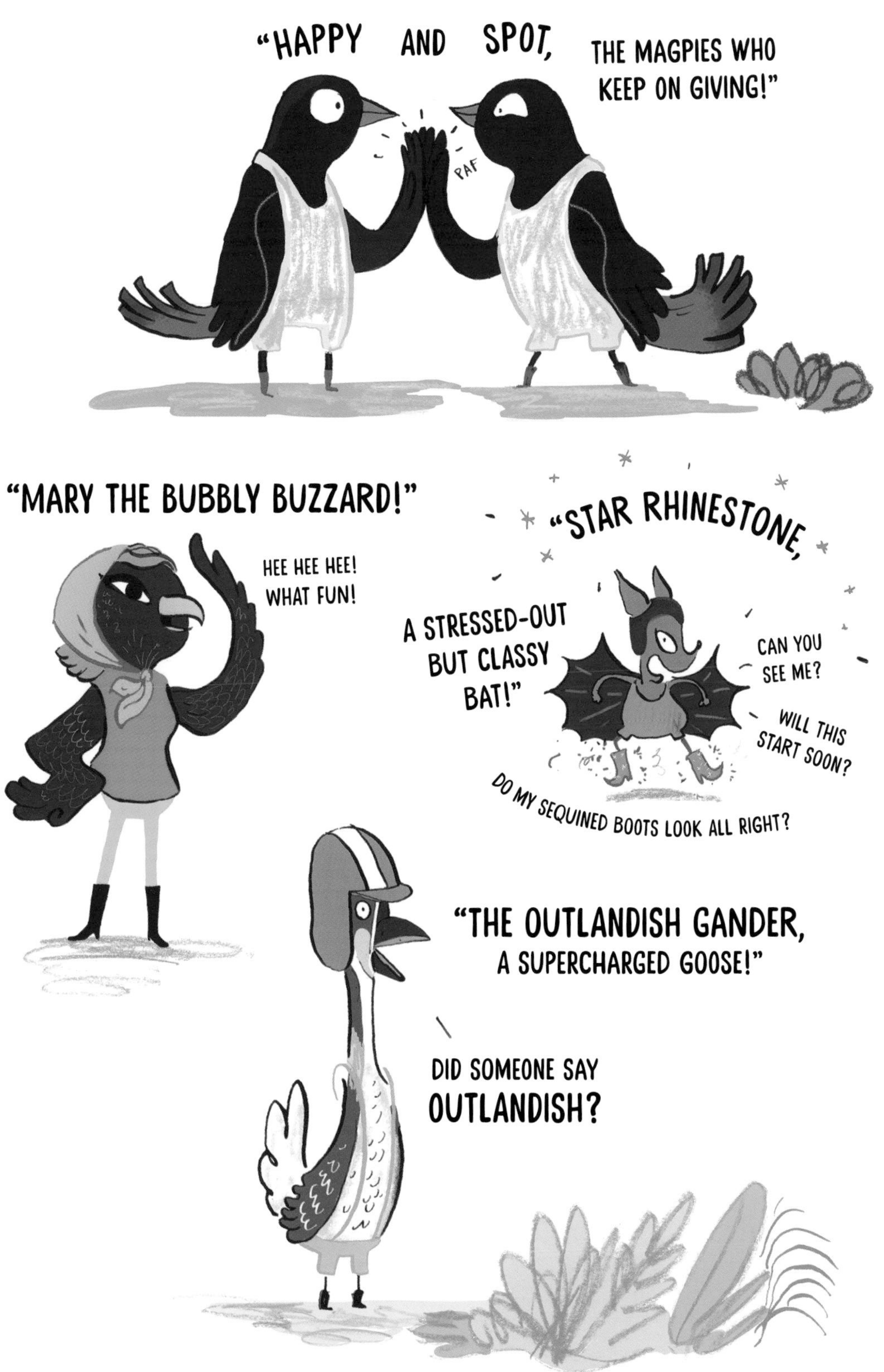
"HAPPY AND SPOT, THE MAGPIES WHO KEEP ON GIVING!"
PAF
"MARY THE BUBBLY BUZZARD!"
HEE HEE HEE! WHAT FUN!
"STAR RHINESTONE, A STRESSED-OUT BUT CLASSY BAT!"
CAN YOU SEE ME?
WILL THIS START SOON?
DO MY SEQUINED BOOTS LOOK ALL RIGHT?
"THE OUTLANDISH GANDER, A SUPERCHARGED GOOSE!"
DID SOMEONE SAY OUTLANDISH?

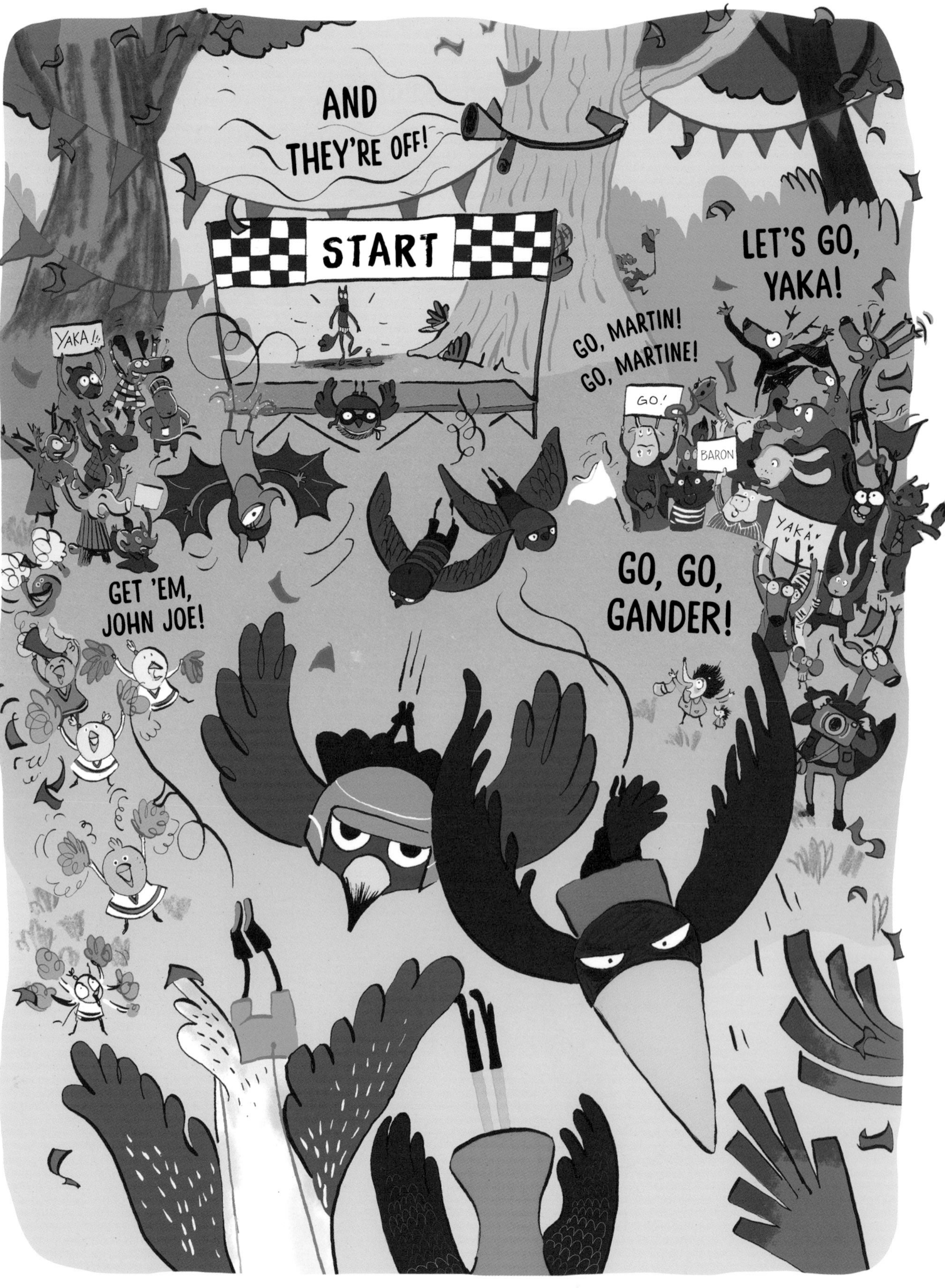
AND THEY'RE OFF!
START
YAKA!!
GO, MARTIN! GO, MARTINE!
LET'S GO, YAKA!
GO!
BARON
YAKA
GET 'EM, JOHN JOE!
GO, GO, GANDER!

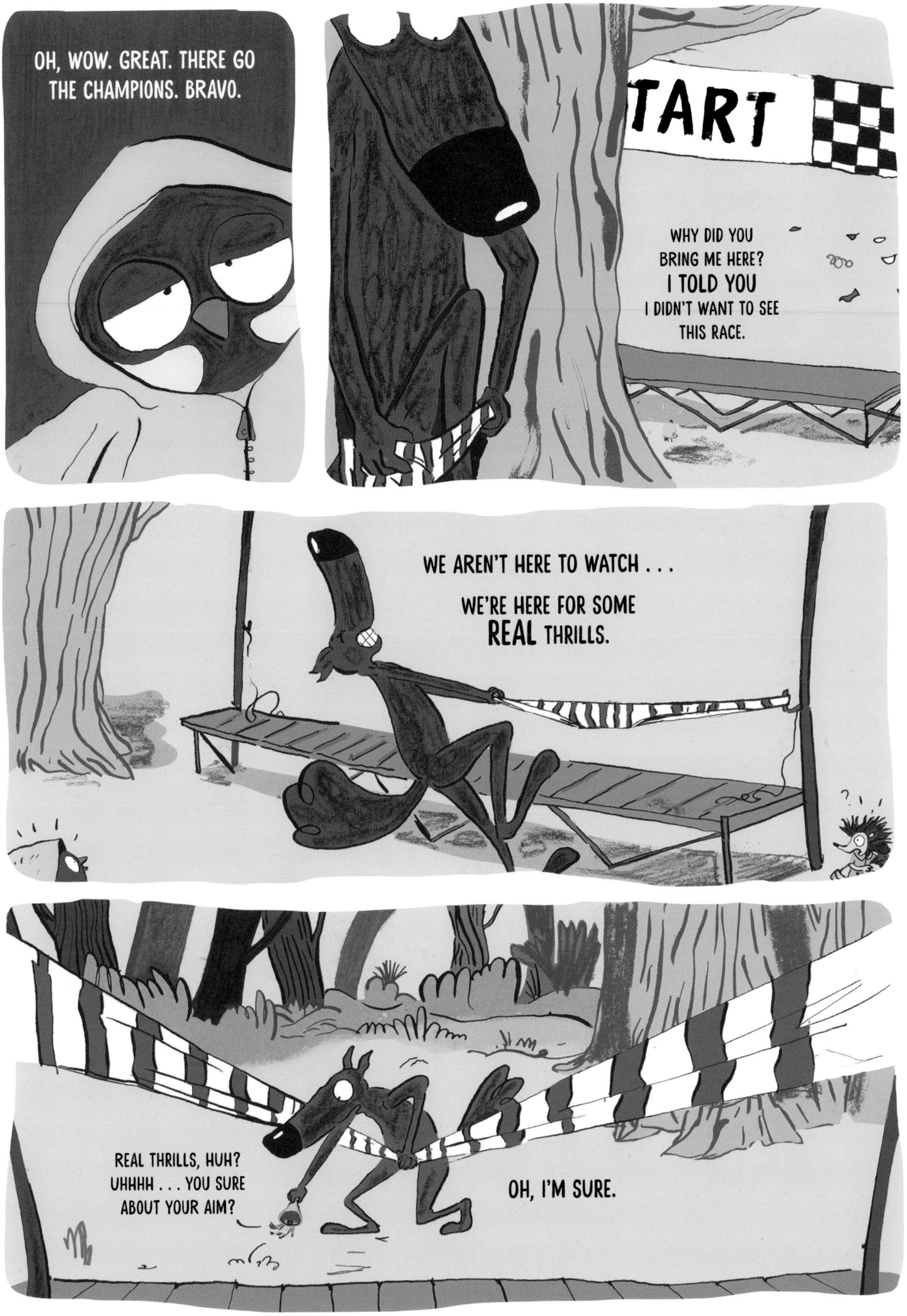
OH, WOW. GREAT. THERE GO THE CHAMPIONS. BRAVO.
TART
WHY DID YOU BRING ME HERE? I TOLD YOU I DIDN'T WANT TO SEE THIS RACE.
WE AREN'T HERE TO WATCH . . .
WE'RE HERE FOR SOME REAL THRILLS.
REAL THRILLS, HUH? UHHHH . . . YOU SURE ABOUT YOUR AIM?
OH, I'M SURE.

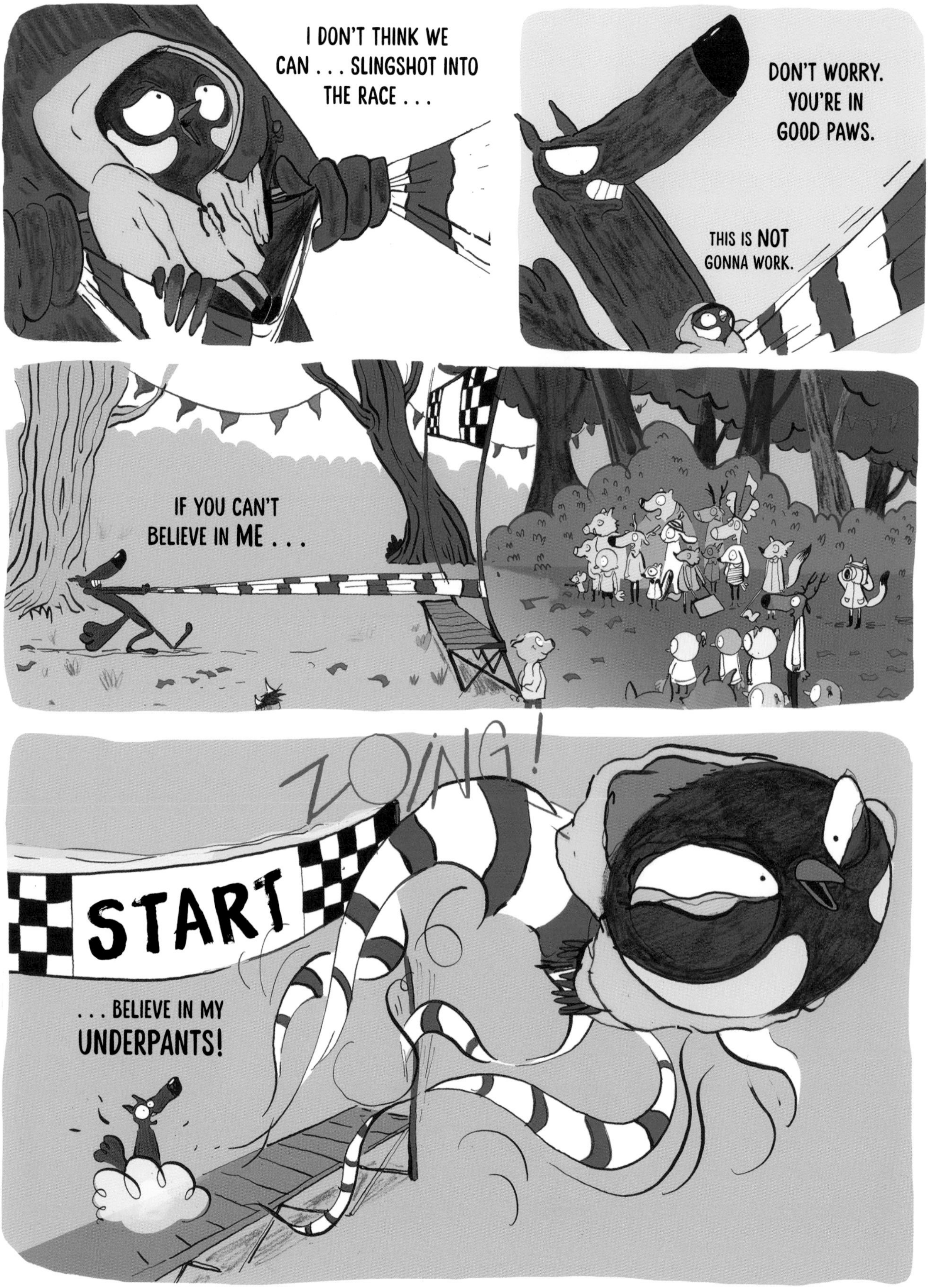
I DON'T THINK WE CAN . . . SLINGSHOT INTO THE RACE . . .
DON'T WORRY. YOU'RE IN GOOD PAWS.
THIS IS NOT GONNA WORK.
IF YOU CAN'T BELIEVE IN ME . . .
ZOING!
START
. . . BELIEVE IN MY UNDERPANTS!

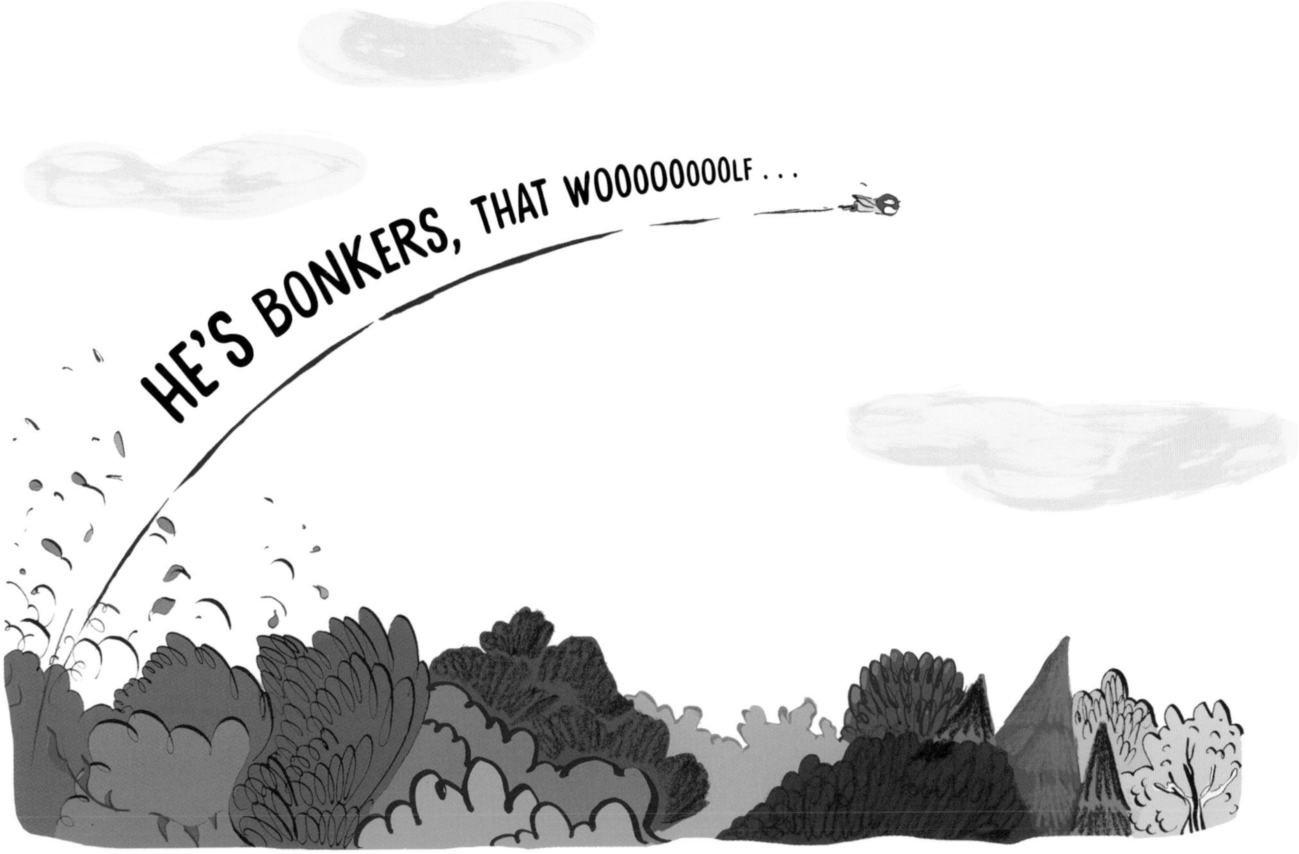
HE'S BONKERS, THAT WOOOOOOOOLF . . .

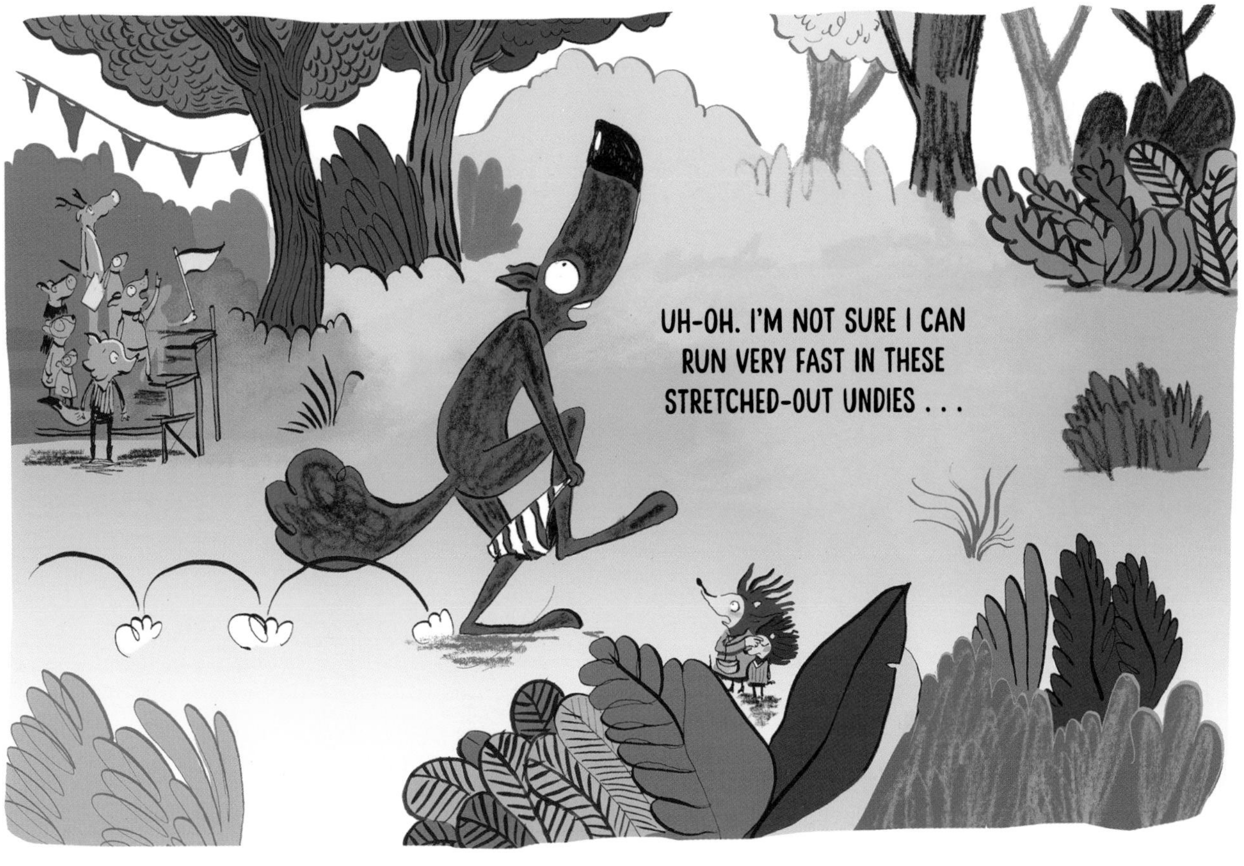
UH-OH. I'M NOT SURE I CAN RUN VERY FAST IN THESE STRETCHED-OUT UNDIES . . .

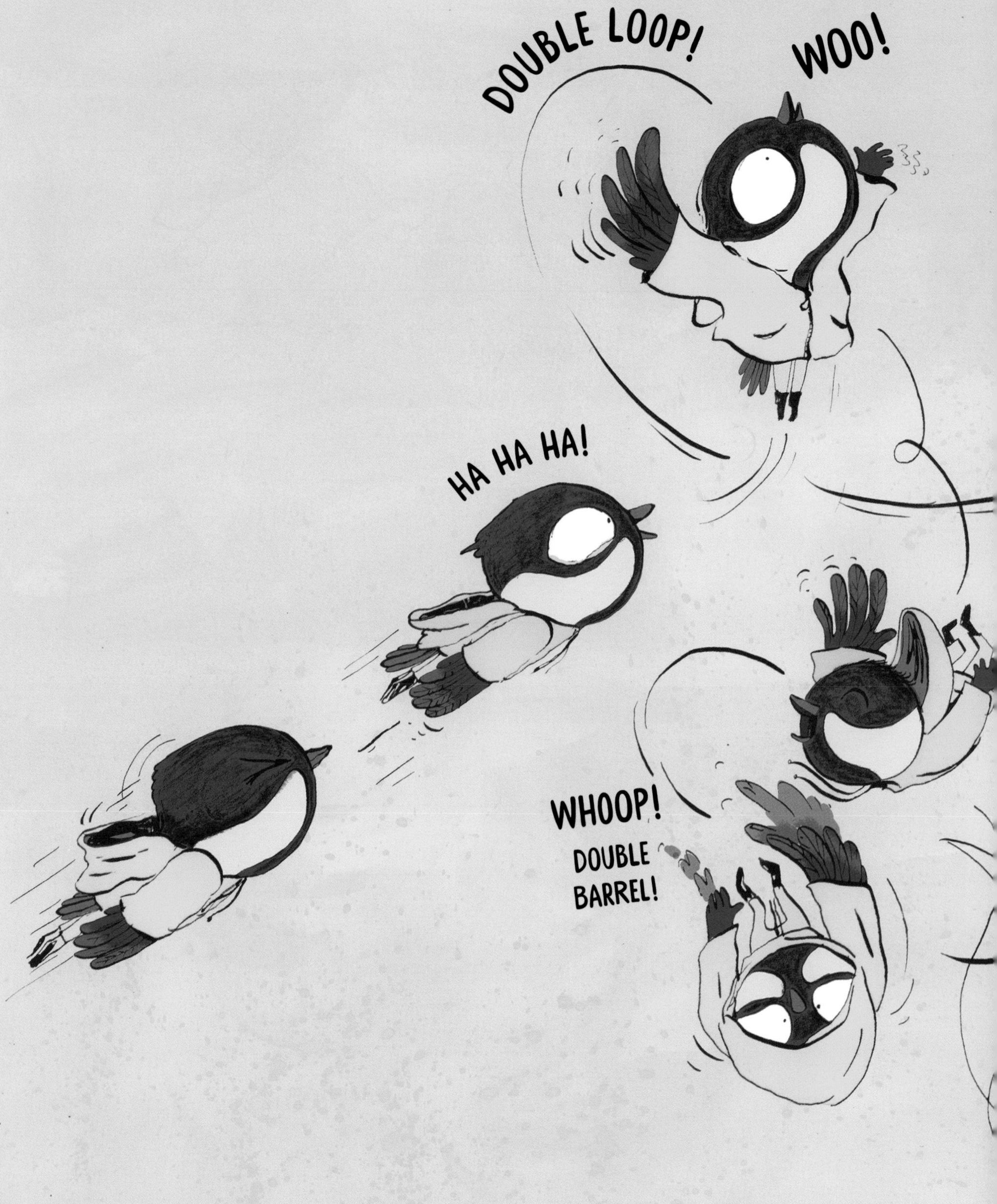
DOUBLE LOOP!
WOO!
HA HA HA!
WHOOP!
DOUBLE BARREL!

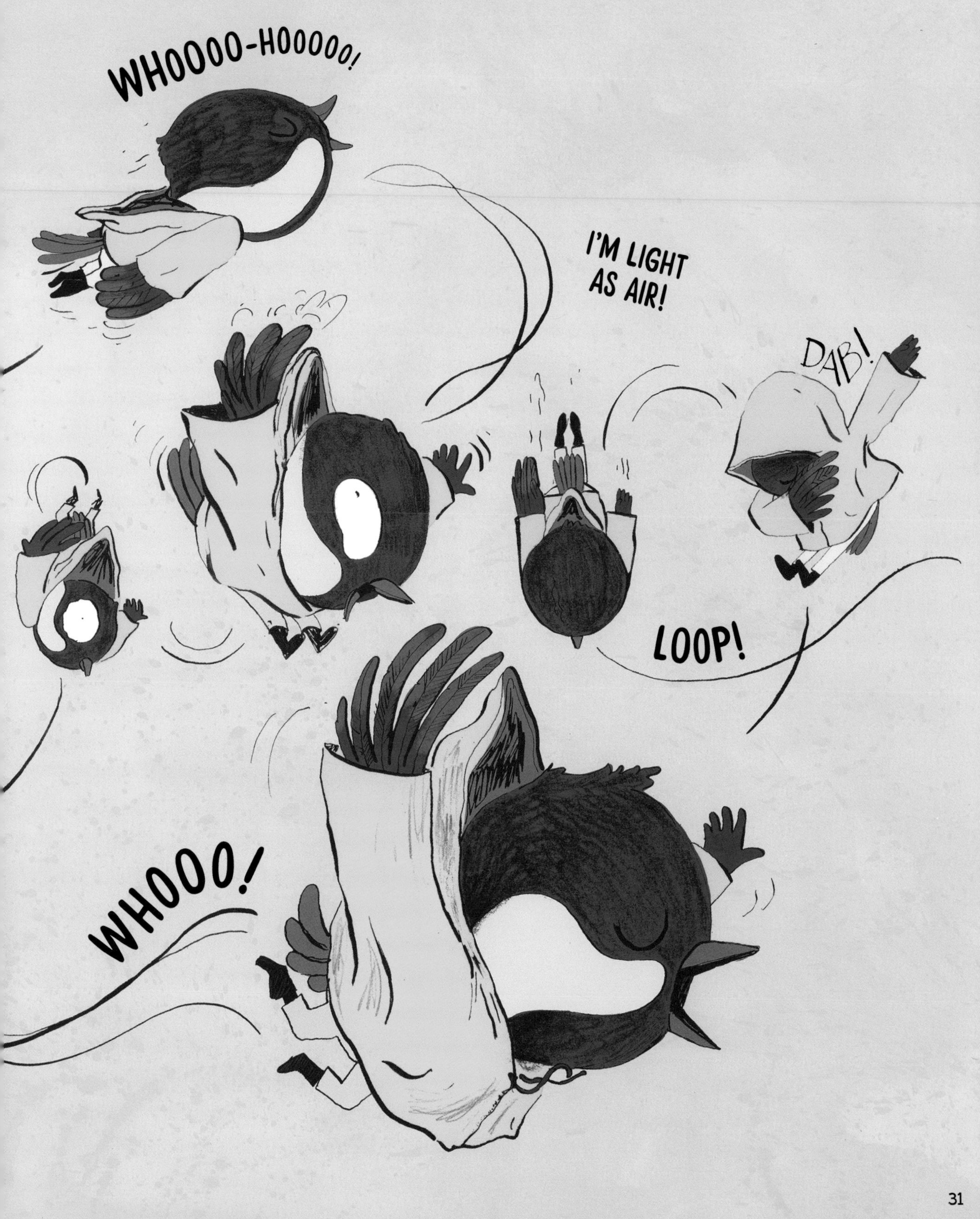
WHOOOO-HOOOOO!
I'M LIGHT AS AIR!
DAB!
LOOP!
WHOOO!

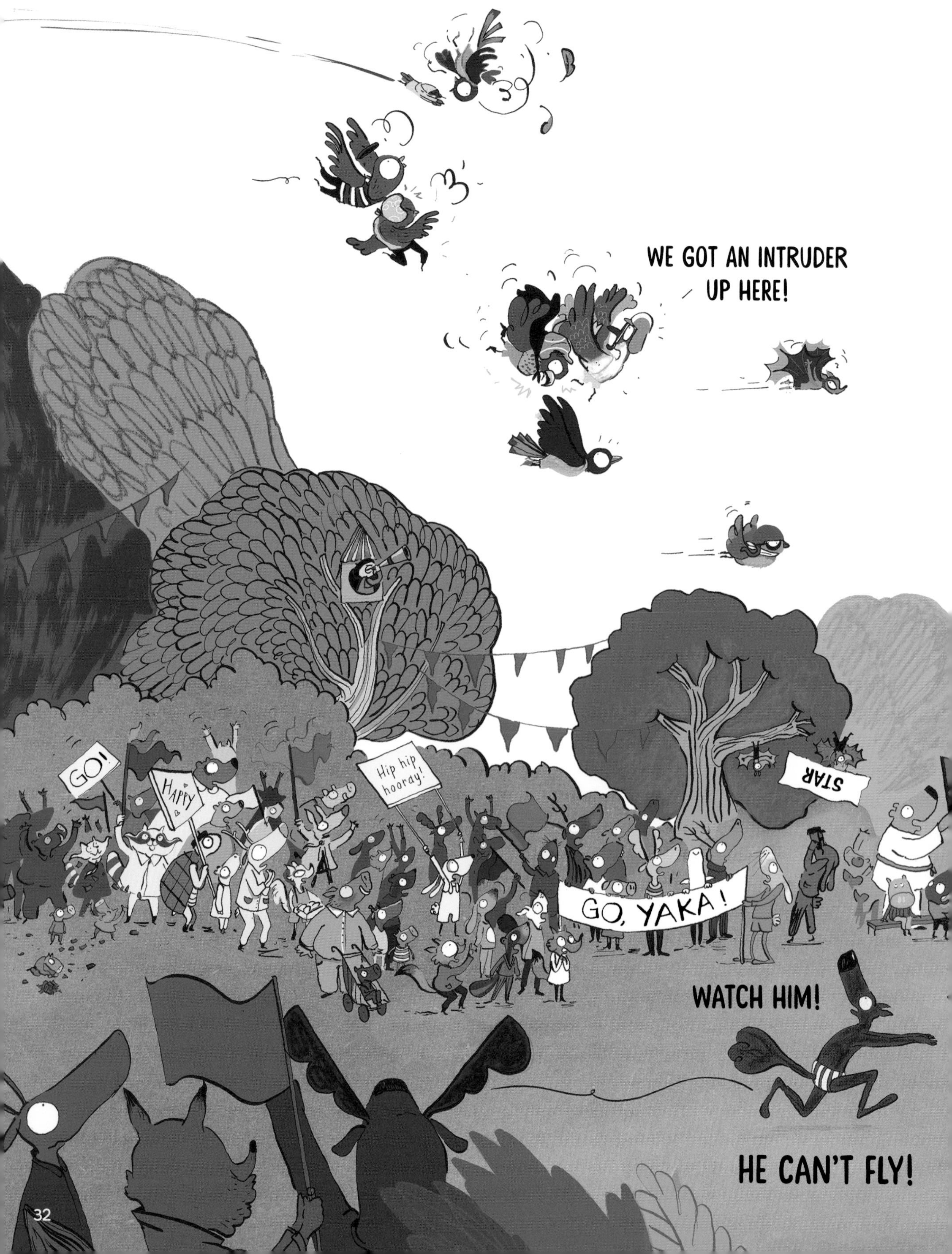
WE GOT AN INTRUDER UP HERE!
GO!
HAPPY
Hip hip hooray!
STAR
GO, YAKA!
WATCH HIM!
HE CAN'T FLY!

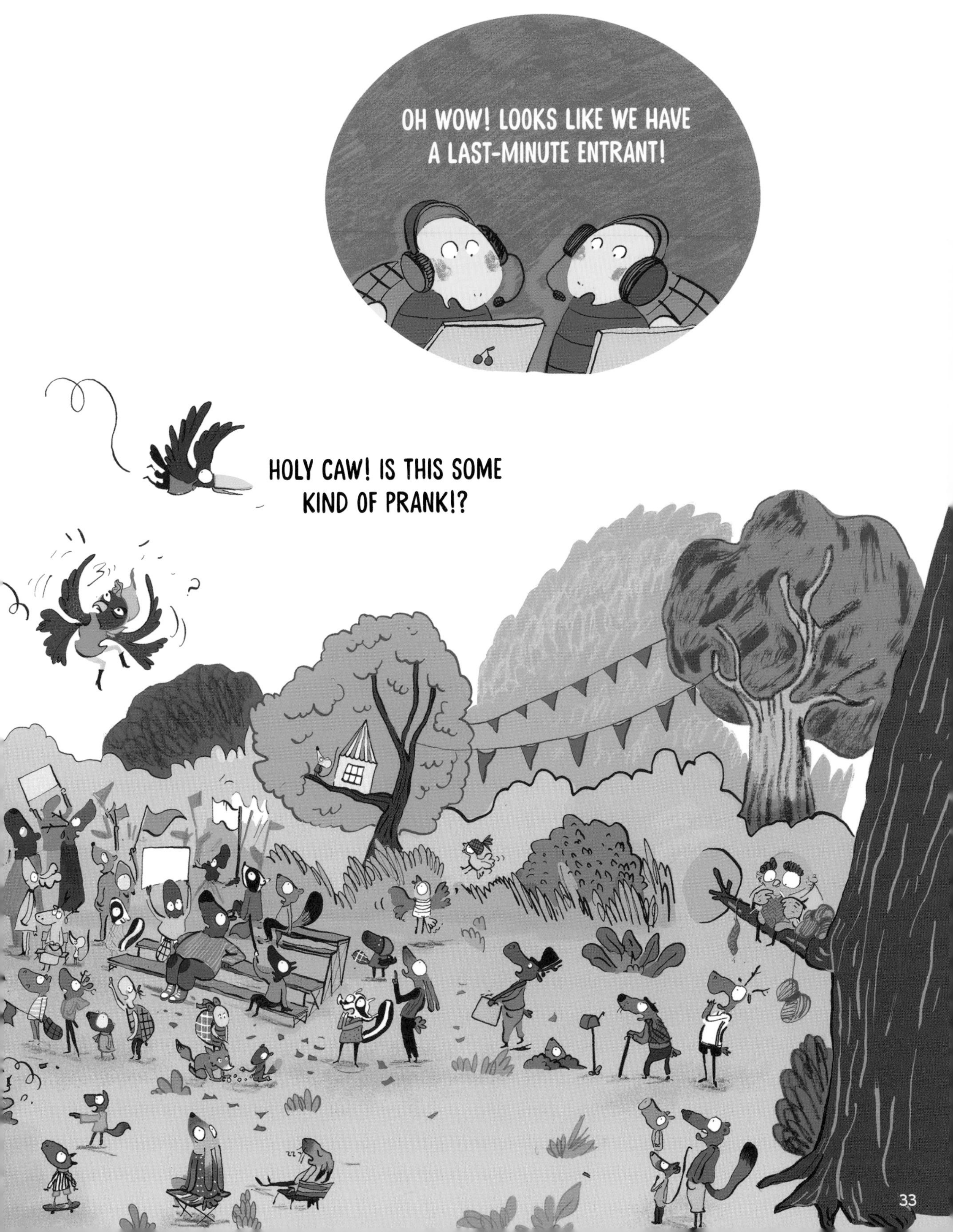
OH WOW! LOOKS LIKE WE HAVE A LAST-MINUTE ENTRANT!
HOLY CAW! IS THIS SOME KIND OF PRANK!?

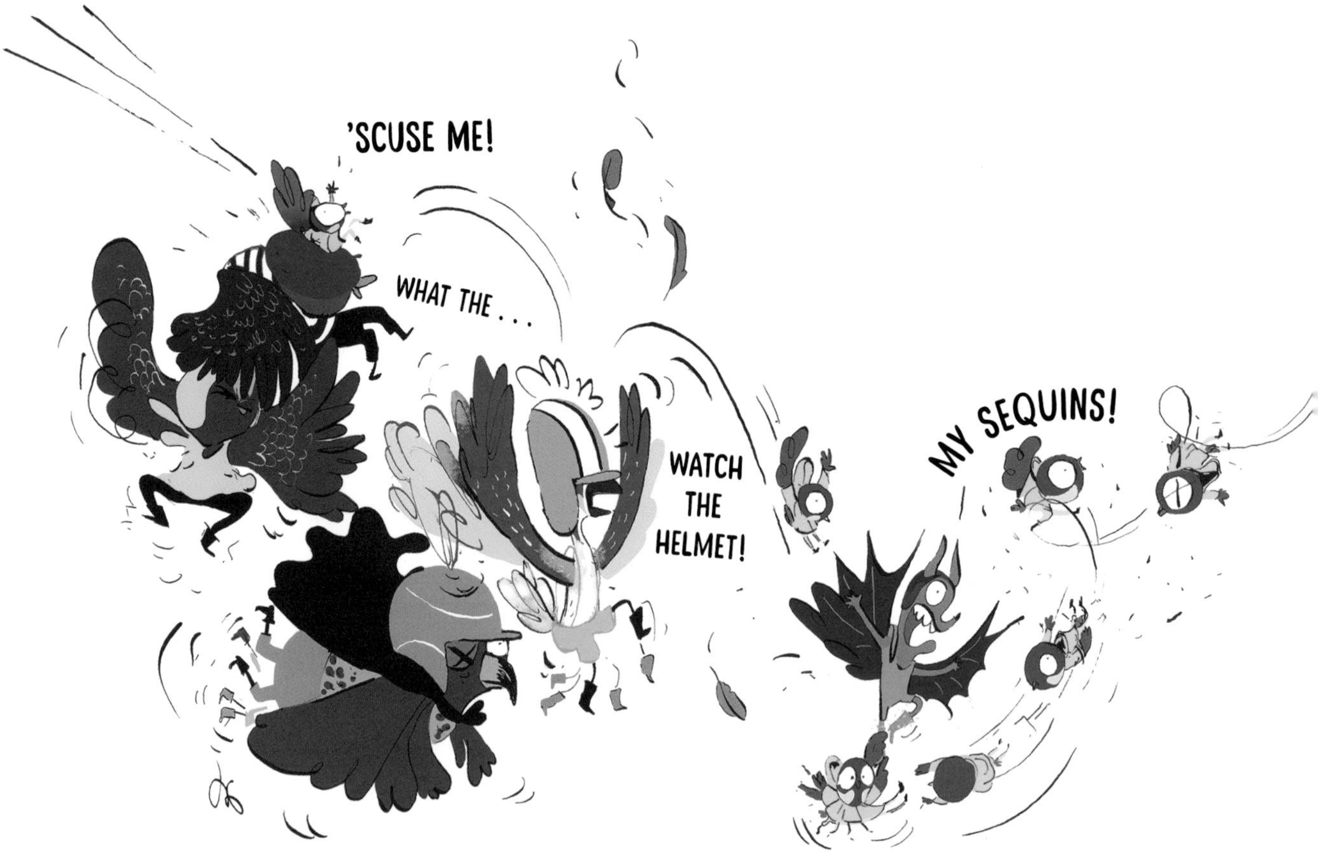
'SCUSE ME!
WHAT THE . . .
WATCH THE HELMET!
MY SEQUINS!

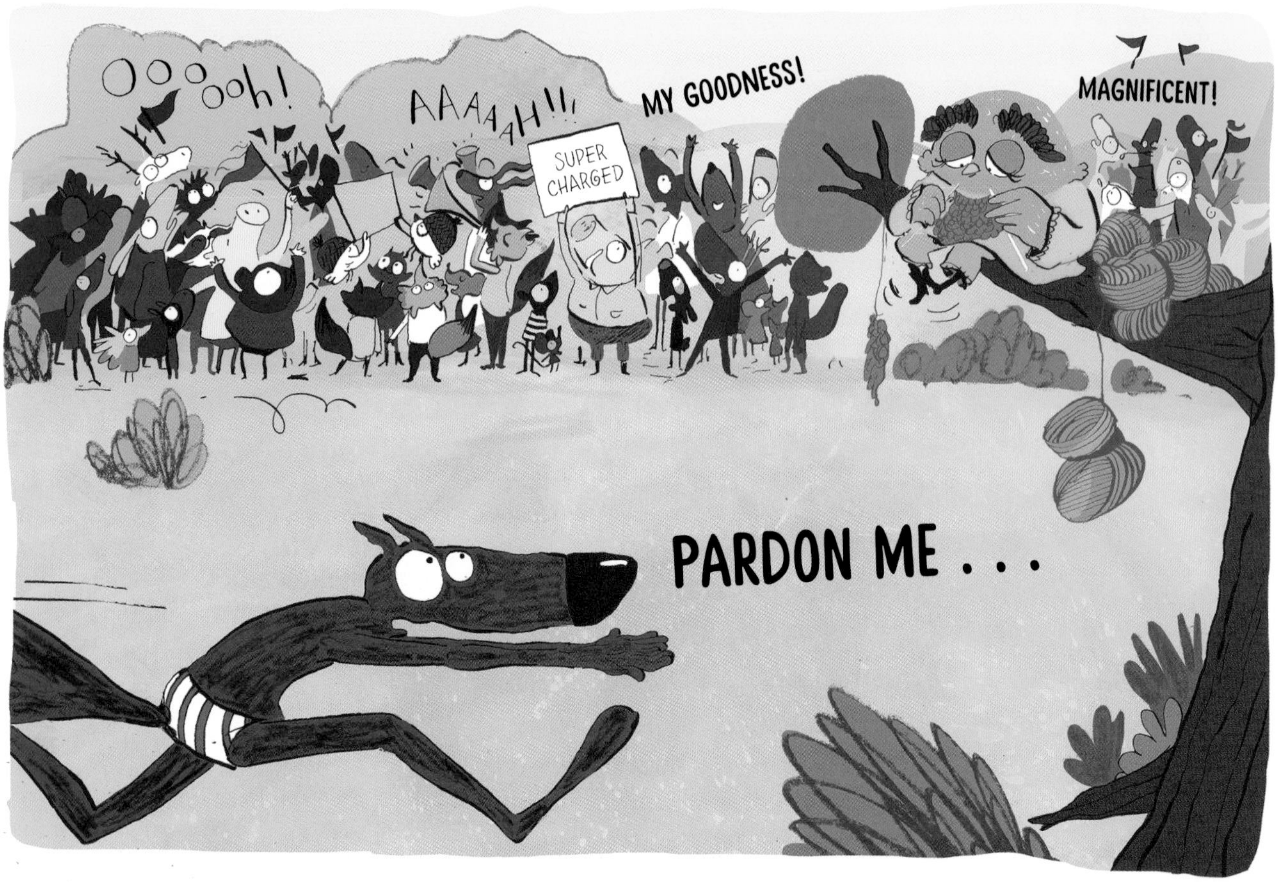
OOOOoh!
AAAAAH!!!
SUPER CHARGED
MY GOODNESS!
MAGNIFICENT!
PARDON ME . . .

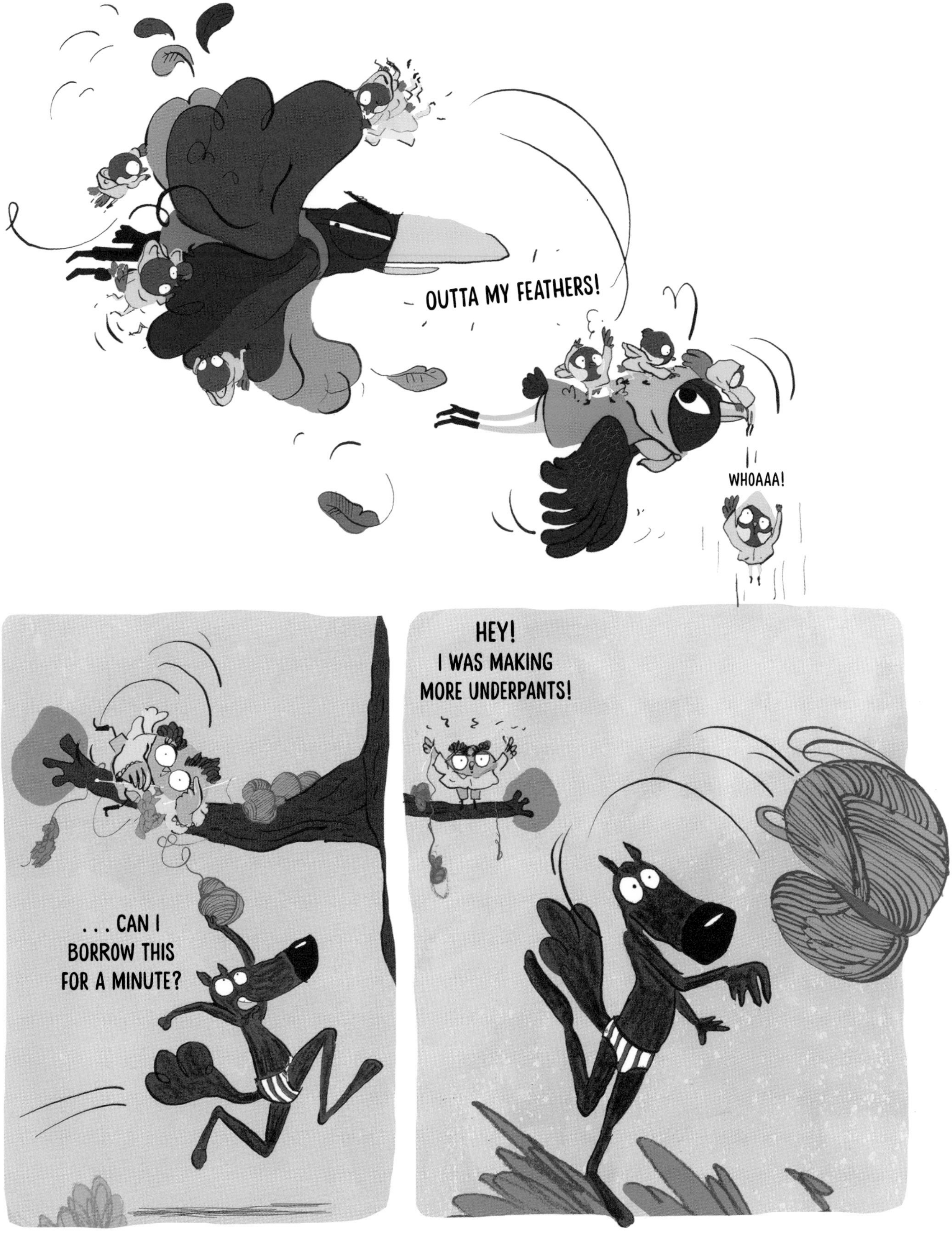
OUTTA MY FEATHERS!
WHOAAA!
. . . CAN I BORROW THIS FOR A MINUTE?
HEY! I WAS MAKING MORE UNDERPANTS!

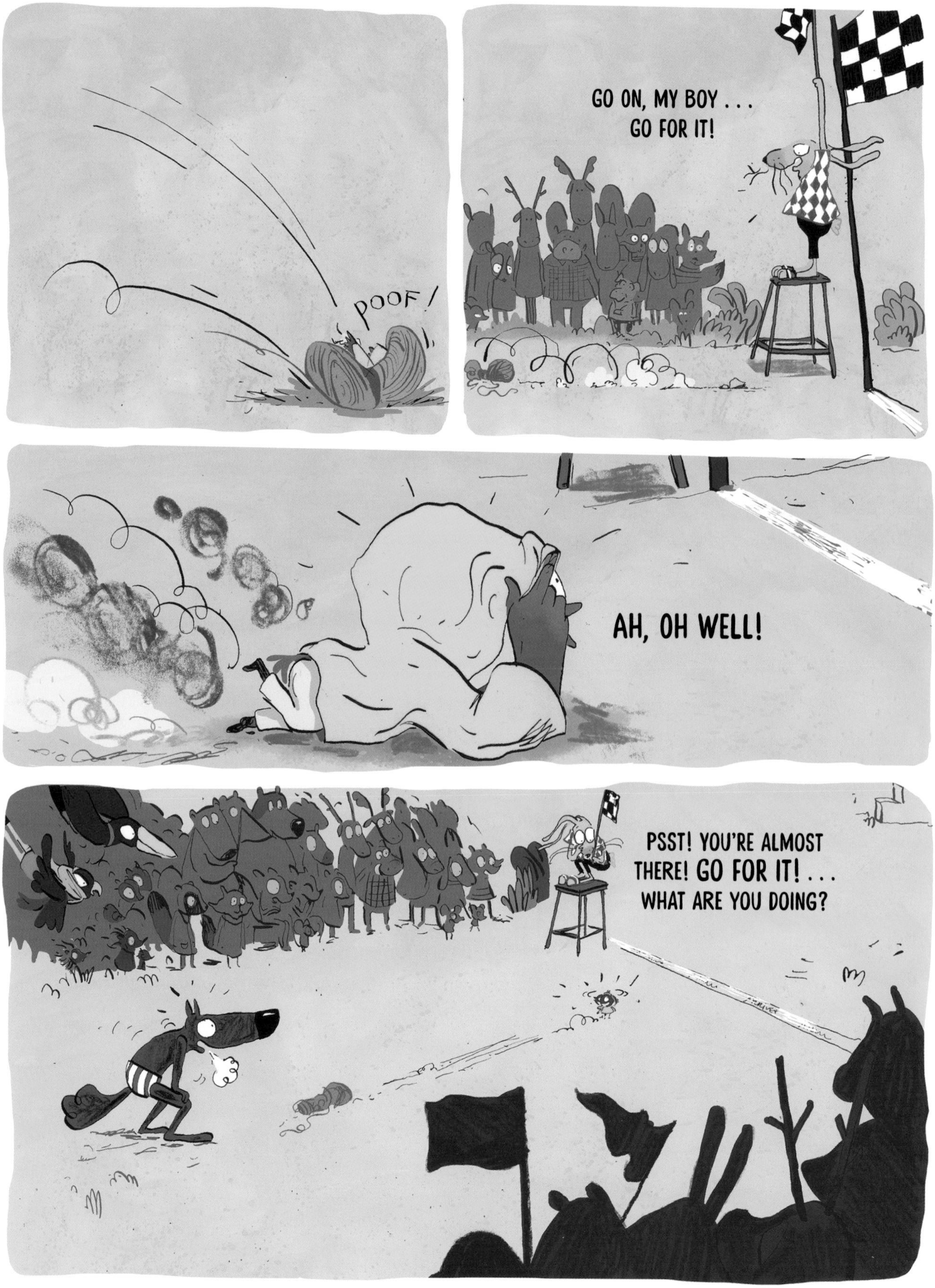
POOF!
GO ON, MY BOY . . . GO FOR IT!
AH, OH WELL!
PSST! YOU'RE ALMOST THERE! GO FOR IT! . . . WHAT ARE YOU DOING?

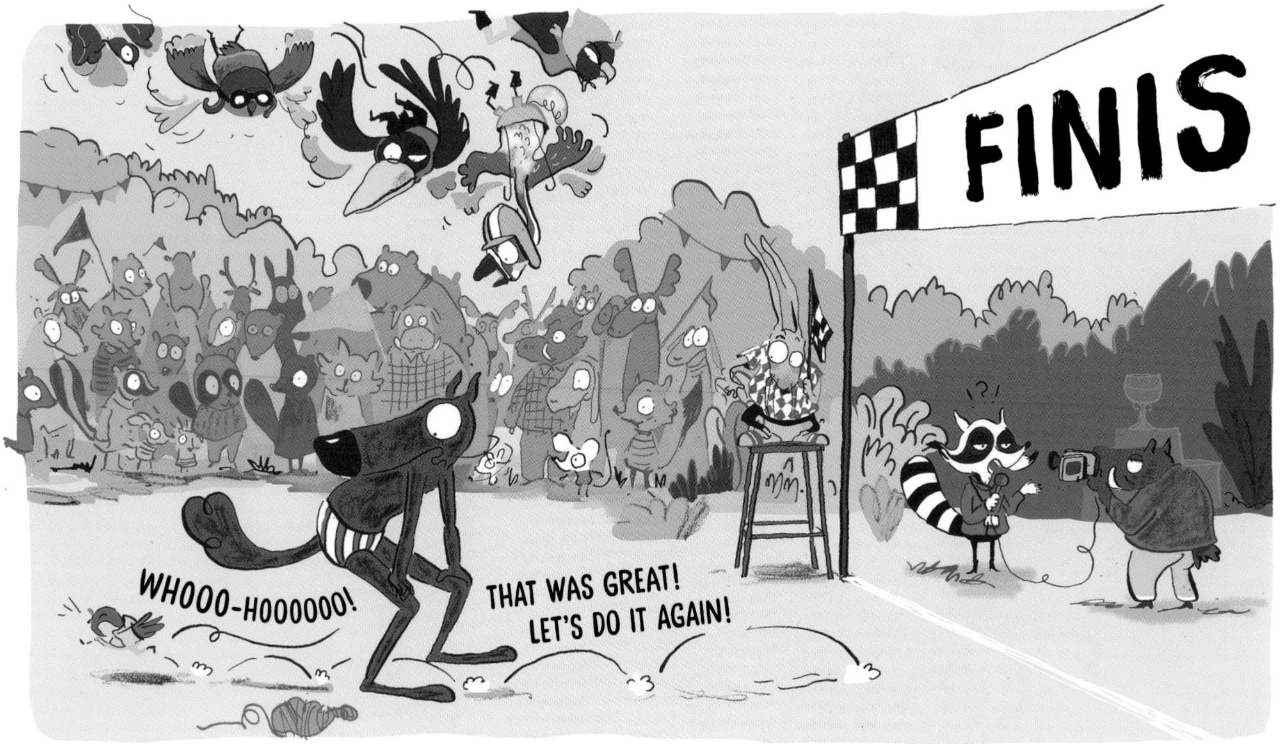
FINIS
!?!
WHOOO-HOOOOOO!
THAT WAS GREAT!
LET'S DO IT AGAIN!

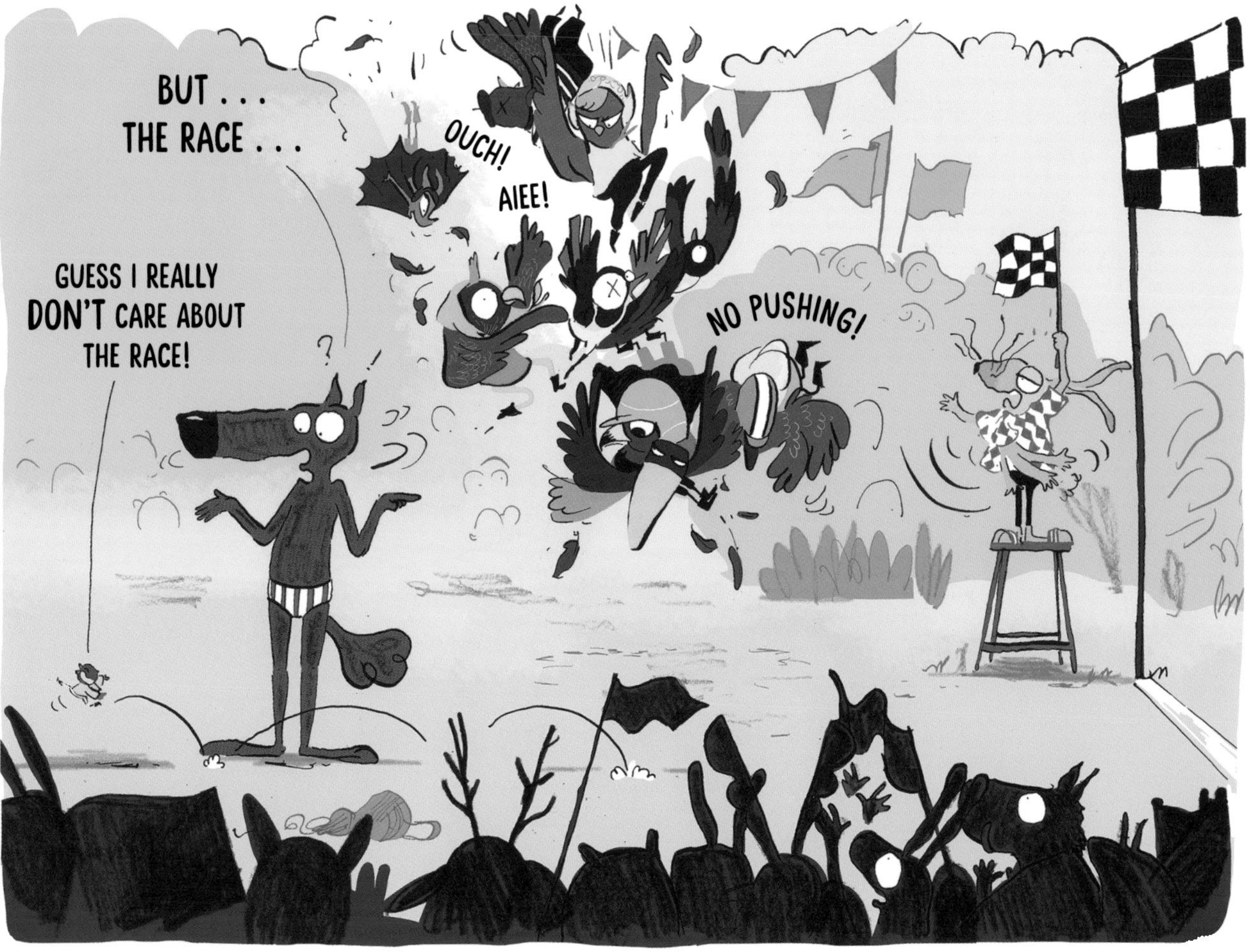
BUT . . .
THE RACE . . .
OUCH!
AIEE!
GUESS I REALLY DON'T CARE ABOUT THE RACE!
NO PUSHING!

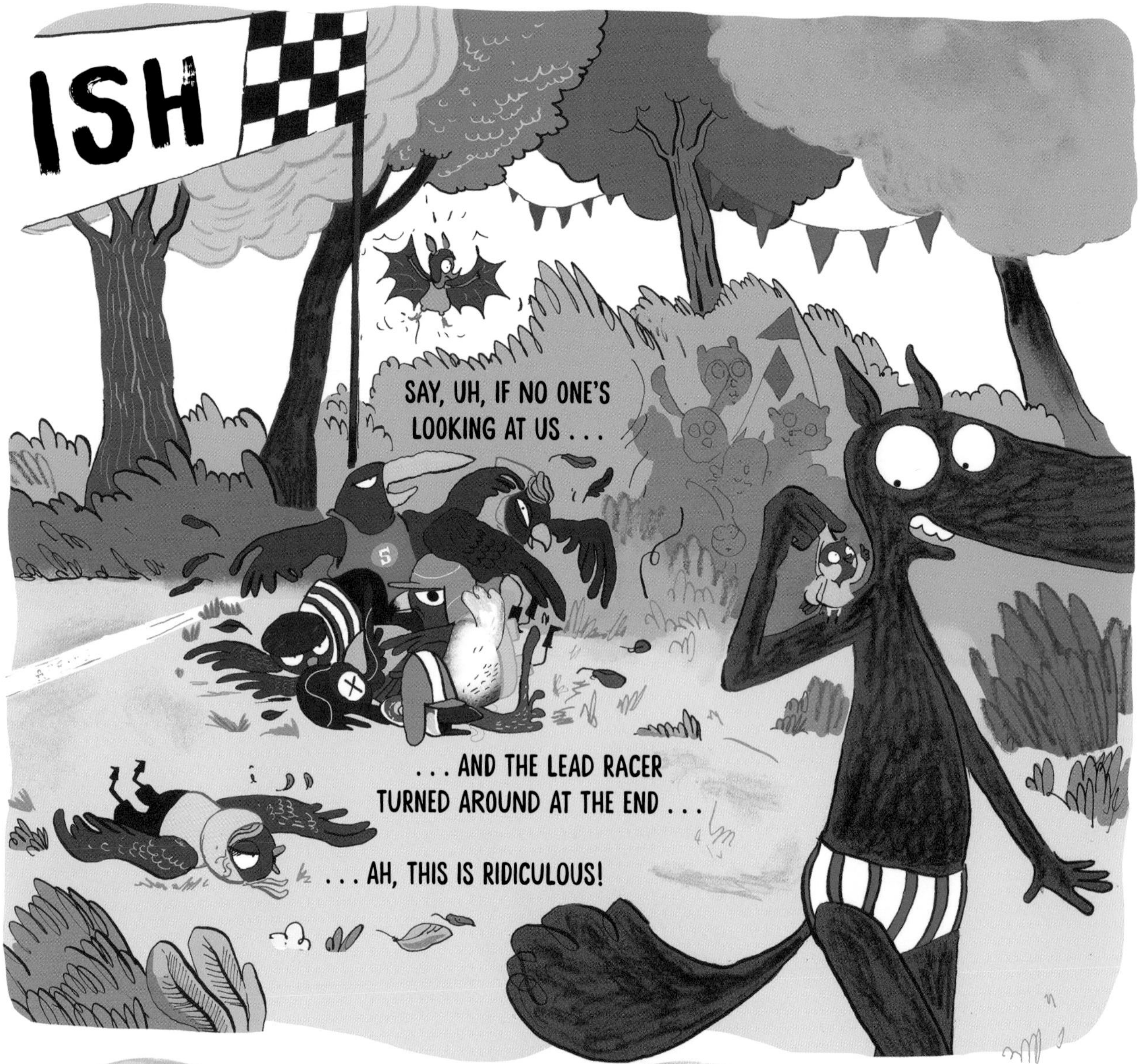
ISH
SAY, UH, IF NO ONE'S LOOKING AT US . . .
. . . AND THE LEAD RACER TURNED AROUND AT THE END . . .
. . . AH, THIS IS RIDICULOUS!

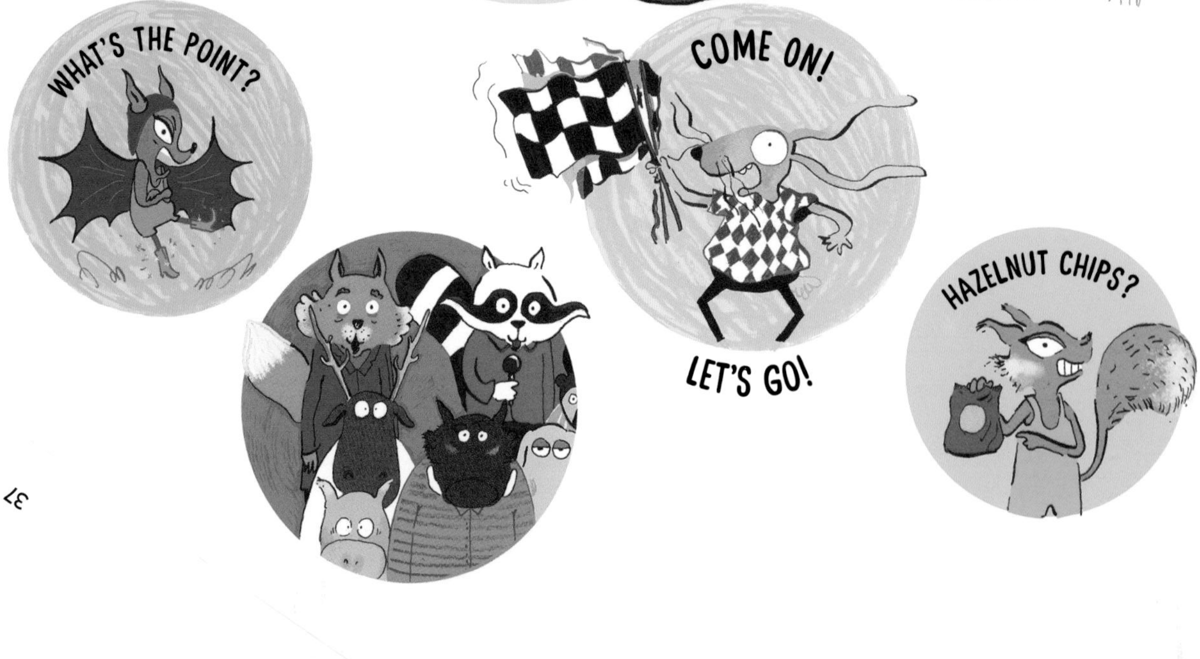
WHAT'S THE POINT?
COME ON!
LET'S GO!
HAZELNUT CHIPS?

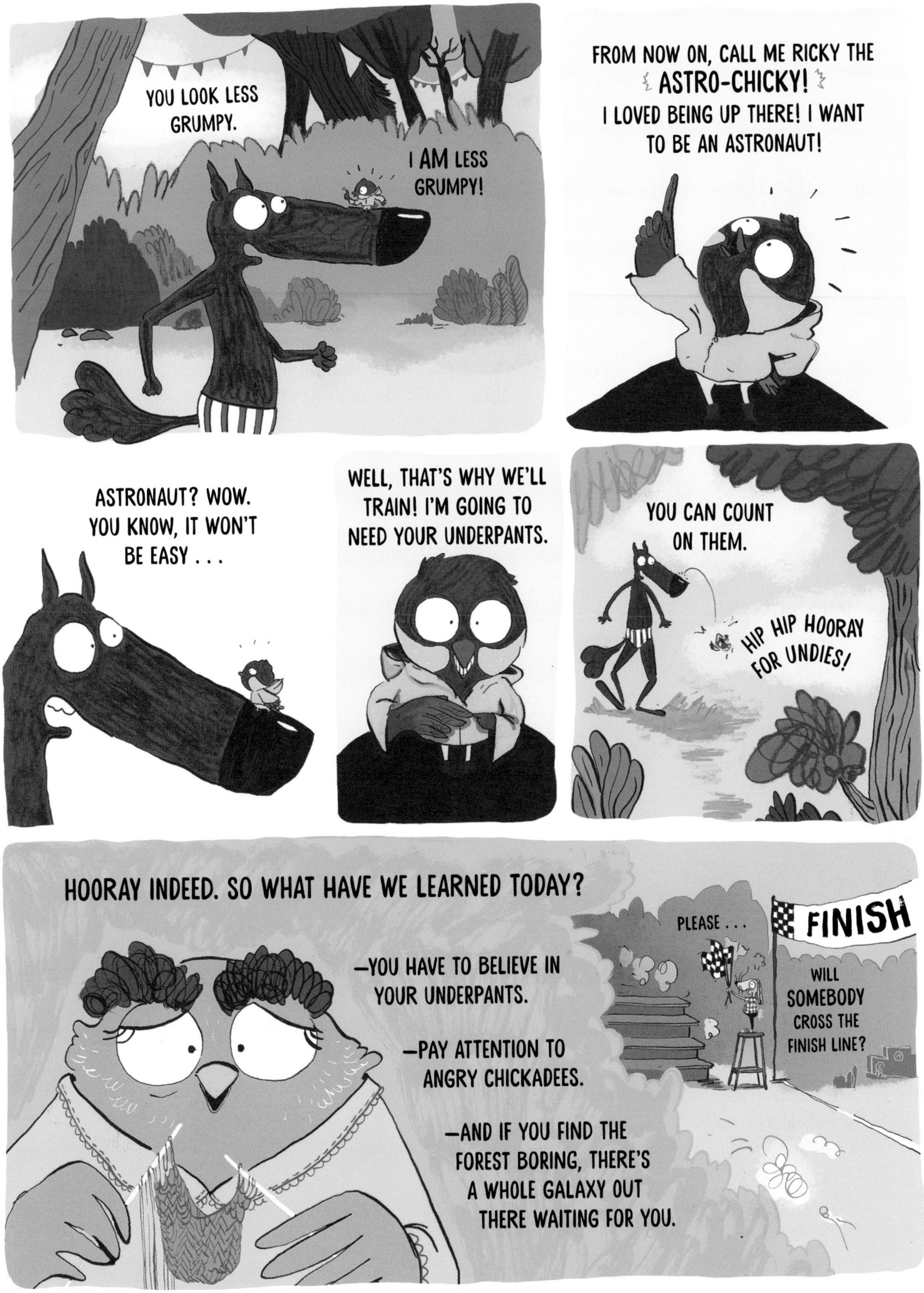
YOU LOOK LESS GRUMPY.
I AM LESS GRUMPY!
FROM NOW ON, CALL ME RICKY THE ASTRO-CHICKY!
I LOVED BEING UP THERE! I WANT TO BE AN ASTRONAUT!
ASTRONAUT? WOW. YOU KNOW, IT WON'T BE EASY . . .
WELL, THAT'S WHY WE'LL TRAIN! I'M GOING TO NEED YOUR UNDERPANTS.
YOU CAN COUNT ON THEM.
HIP HIP HOORAY FOR UNDIES!
HOORAY INDEED. SO WHAT HAVE WE LEARNED TODAY?
—YOU HAVE TO BELIEVE IN YOUR UNDERPANTS.
—PAY ATTENTION TO ANGRY CHICKADEES.
—AND IF YOU FIND THE FOREST BORING, THERE'S A WHOLE GALAXY OUT THERE WAITING FOR YOU.
PLEASE . . .
FINISH
WILL SOMEBODY CROSS THE FINISH LINE?

ABOUT THE CREATORS

WILFRID LUPANO

Wilfrid Lupano was born in Nantes, in the west of France, and spent most of his childhood in the southwestern city of Pau, France. He spent his childhood reading through his parents' comic book collection and enjoying role-playing games. He studied literature and philosophy, receiving a degree in English, before he began to script comics. He has written numerous graphic novels for French readers, including the series *Les Vieux Fourneaux* (in English, *The Old Geezers*). With this series, Lupano and Paul Cauuet first developed the idea that would become *The Wolf in Underpants*. Lupano once again lives in Pau after spending several years in the city of Toulouse.

MAYANA ITOÏZ

Mayana Itoïz was born in the city of Bayonne, in the southwest of France, and studied at the institut supérieur des arts de Toulouse (School of Fine Arts in Toulouse), where she worked in many different mediums. In addition to being an illustrator and a cartoonist, she has taught art to high school students. She lives in the Pyrenees, near France's mountainous southern border, and splits her time between art, family, and travel.

PAUL CAUUET

Paul Cauuet was born in Toulouse and grew up in a family that encouraged his passion for drawing. He was also a fond reader of classic Franco-Belgian comics such as *Tintin* and *Asterix*. He studied at the University of Toulouse and went on to a career as a cartoonist. Cauuet and Wilfrid Lupano first collaborated on an outer-space comedy series before working together on *Les Vieux Fourneaux* (*The Old Geezers*).

ABOUT THE TRANSLATOR

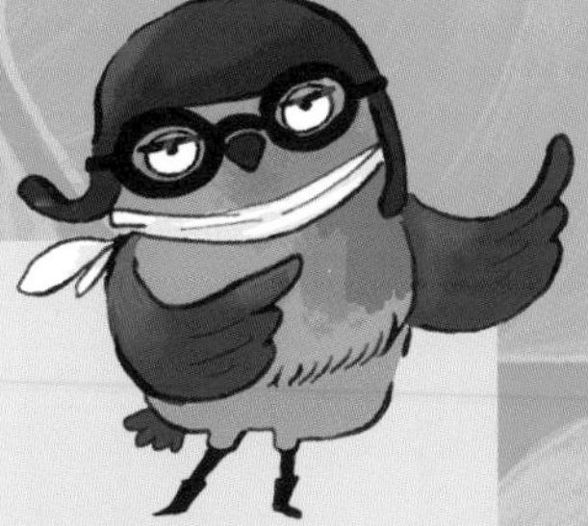

NATHAN SACKS

Nathan Sacks is a writer, editor, and translator from Ames, Iowa, who lives in Los Angeles. He has written fiction and nonfiction children's books and translated several graphic novels from French to English.

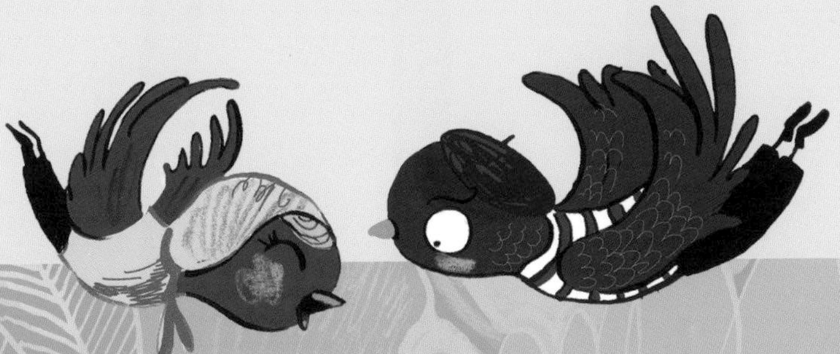

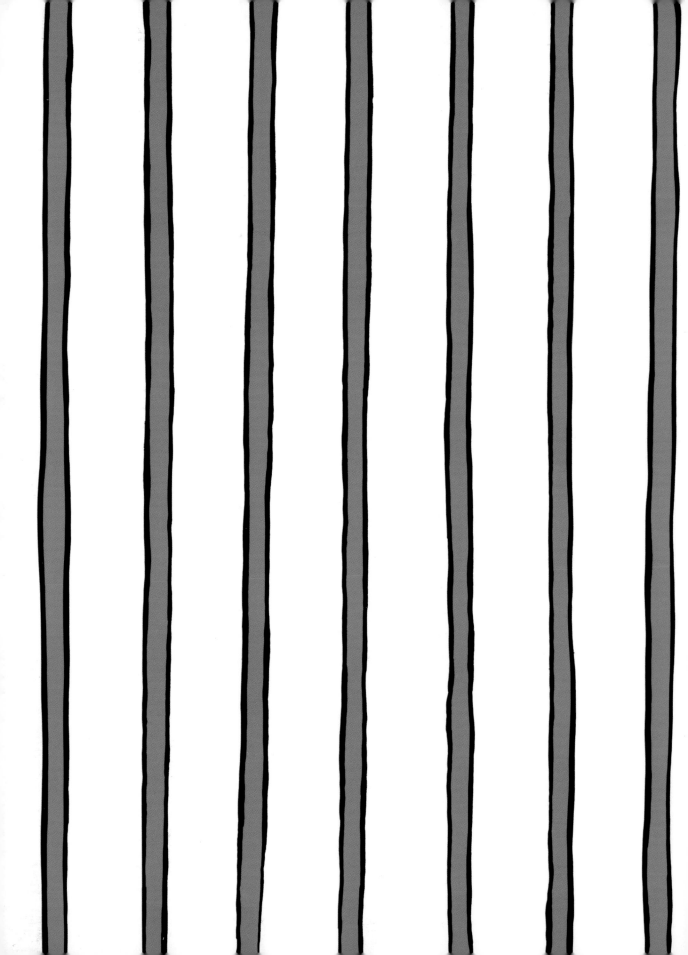